BLACKWOOD

A GOTHEIM TALE

CLYDE DAVIS

CLYDE DAVIS

This edition published 2019 by Clyde Davis.

ISBN: 978 0 620 84040 8

Copyright © 2019 by Clyde Davis

For those who strive to be something else.

CONTENTS

INTRODUCTION

The inquisitor Blackwood and the grim spires and alleyways of Gotheim emerged from the shadowy reaches of my mind not as a result of a deliberate attempt to create either one. Rather, I found myself at a point in my life, balanced precariously between a professional career and the hungering desire to write each day, whilst facing the ultimate obstacle of time. There was not enough time to do the latter. Not in the sense that I believed was constructive or redeeming. I haunted moments in-between tasks at the office trying to make use of time to write something; or I lingered over the keyboard during the evenings, my exhausted mind struggling to exhume anything encouraging from the dregs of the day. I was unsatisfied with my attempts. I was displeased with what small pieces of writing I had started to collect. Little bodies of work that lay incomplete and forsaken on the pile.

In an effort to offset this and to ultimately create a habit of writing that would encourage me to continue, I began to allocate particular evenings to writing isolated tales. Stories that would begin and end. That way, removing the pressure from myself to nurture complicated narratives and plots. The point was to relax, write and imagine. The exercise proved fruitful, and in a span of time shorter than I would've expected, I was developing a flowing work ethic and generating short tales that I was proud of. It was a surprise to me though, of the nature of these tales. Unlike the lifelong inspirations of *Middle-Earth* and *The Wheel of Time*, my tales strayed from the well-worn paths of the epic fantasy realms. Instead, I found myself wandering through gloom and fog. What emerged from this darkened place were wildly haunted forests, nightmarish hinterlands and cities of pandemonium. Along the horizon arose a fist of spires, black and ancient, and behind the grotesque walls of that vast city, at the heart of the ocean of towers and spires I found the Citadel. It was from that great fortress-tower that Marcus Blackwood emerged.

Quite simply, and quickly, Blackwood imposed himself upon the series of isolated tales I was writing. His dark, wolfish figure strode through my writings, becoming a centre piece for much of what I imagined and wrote. It seemed only natural that I accepted his influence and allowed him to be my guide through the darkness of Gotheim. Horrors and nightmares surrounded him, and yet he strode onward, unperturbed by what evil the world of Gotheim had to throw at him. This was the original seed for developing Blackwood and the world of Gotheim into a workable series. Much like the anti-hero figure of so many other works which have preceded this one, I wished to explore the flawed nature of an individual who had the power (or rather the ability) to save the world, and yet be utterly incapable of redeeming themselves. Blackwood is this figure. A man who has defeated darkness. A man who remains in its shadow. A hero who can no longer see the light. These are the dynamics that drive the looming figure of the aged inquisitor.

This debut novel of the *Gotheim* series is but a touch upon the surface of a lake with vast, insidious depths. This is an introduction to Blackwood and the dark realm of Gotheim. Will you join me as the Citadel battles against the resurgence of the ancient *Old Ways*?

- Clyde Davis, July 1, 2019

1

THE INQUISITOR

The autumn morning was colder than usual. The forerunner of the winter winds had already arrived from the south bringing with it a thick front of cloud and rain. Despite the conditions, the streets surrounding the vast train terminal teemed with people. The terminal's vast dome reached into the imposing clouds overhead, its highest point disappearing into the grey murk. Along the ring of the dome great statues of battle-ready angels—armoured and armed—leered down from their gloomy perches. The shadows cast by the dampening clouds twisted the heavenly faces into masks of judgement and their angelic wings seemed tattered and filthy. The line of holy statues were apocalyptic in the failing weather. A strong gust of wind blew from the south, bringing with it the stench of the Unclean Quarter. The cold and the clarity in the air after rainfall sharpened the stench. Notes of filth, waste and old smoke followed on the back of the southerly wind, leaving the wretched smell of the slum's forsaken over the station.

On a street corner across from the train station Marcus Blackwood watched as tongues of people moved in and out of the arched entrances to the terminal. He found satisfaction in how the nature of the throng ignored the firm castes of the city. In the teeming mass, all were equal, and the poor brushed shoulders with the refined. Peddlers lined the streets, calling and yelling, as they offered their wares to the disinterested clamour of people. To the right, a group of priests clung to the foot of an angelic statue, as if it were a bulwark against the tide of people, and distributed pamphlets of the Church. The unwashed and desperate bowed at their feet and tugged humbly at the hems of their robes as they begged for blessings and salvation. Above the scene of priests and poor, the everlasting gaze of the statue peered out to the surrounding city as if it cared little for the woes of mortals.

Blackwood turned away from the priests. He found them righteous and apathetic—just two symptoms of the sickness that had taken hold of the Church. Those desperate souls would find little salvation from the so-called holy men. *Wolves amongst sheep*, he thought. From the shadow cast by his wide-brimmed hat, Blackwood's dark and hardened eyes surveyed the crowd. He watched as a gentleman and lady followed their servicemen through the human traffic, the ushers doggedly clearing a passage for their employers. The crowd parted enough to let the group through, but, by the look of anguish on the lady's face, it was evident she disapproved of her close vicinity to the unwashed. Mud from the rain-soaked streets spoiled the lining of her emerald dress and her honey-brown hair was coming undone from the immaculately crafted bun beneath her teardrop hat. She pressed her oversized handbag to her chest and followed closely behind her husband. Blackwood's eyes tracked the couple and their retinue of servants, as well as the pack of street urchins that stalked them through the crowd. The pack of cutpurses was five strong. Two on the left, and three to right. He followed their hungry eyes to the handbag held by the lady's arms. It would be hard work getting it from her clutches, but Blackwood knew the tenacity of Gotheim's underbelly. By the look of the thieving children, they were vermin from the Unclean Quarter—filthy and as agitated as the rats that flooded the slum's gutters. Skin darkened with dirt and eyes marred with the yellow tinge of malnourishment, they looked like rats too. The urchins wouldn't risk a blatant snatch—not with so many servants and footmen about. They would most probably cause a diversion. *Yes, that's what they'd do*. He'd seen it many times before. Perhaps they'd pester the gentleman, or trip up one of the footman and send luggage sprawling, but either way, in the chaos caused, one of them would pounce on the handbag. Intervention would be easy, Blackwood mused. His mere presence would send the thieves scurrying in retreat, but it wasn't his responsibility. The fate of the fine lady's handbag caused little concern for him. Such trivial matters of doing good and preventing bad were beneath him. This was the responsibility of the constabulary. He looked about the heaving throng and saw no city constables. *Pity*, he thought.

Another southerly wind raked through the busy street, reinvigorating the stink from the Unclean Quarter. The stench would only get worse with the passing of the day as the markets deep within the slums opened for trade and the sickly produce soured in the open air. Blackwood could almost envisage the stray dogs, boney and ragged, scampering from one stall to the next, scavenging for any soiled scraps. He turned his face from the wind and the reinvigorated smell that followed on the back of it, and looked up the street.

Beyond the shifting traffic of people, he could make out the towers and spires of Gotheim disappearing into the distance. The city was an ocean of such structures—tall baroque spikes and reaching fingers that stabbed at the sky.

What was visible to him along the street was a mere glance through a keyhole. The city was vast and far reaching, and yet it felt like a tumour, ripened and ready to rupture. Thousands of refugees had fled to the safety of the city during the wars —its tall walls the only real protection against the horrors that swept through the realm. The wars were over now; they had been for a long time, and yet the people never left the city. Perhaps it was the ease of staying, rather than returning to some blasted plot of land to start over again. There had been no effort by the Council of Suprema to vacate the refugees once peace was established. How could they? Gotheim was the symbol of the emperors' dominion. What message would it send if the Lord Marshal forced the people he was sworn to protect from the emperors' city? He couldn't blame the Lord Marshal entirely. The Church had a role to play in harbouring the refugees too. Just like the Lord Marshal, the Bishop King wished to demonstrate the generosity of the Church. Now, the city was overpopulated. The Unclean Quarter was barely containable and the face of the city was beginning to turn ugly. Blackwood glanced over the crowd again from beneath the brim of his hat and visited a thought he had often. Perhaps the city's gentle accommodation of the refugees was the reason for the swollen population, but he believed there was another reason why those who had fled to the city never returned to their lands, and it was simple—fear. Fear for what still lurked out in the wilderness. Fear of what haunted the darkness beyond the walls of the city, and although no one would risk saying it, Blackwood knew, they were afraid of what may still stalk the streets of Gotheim itself.

He scowled at the people before looking up the street again. In the distance, beyond the spires and towers, deep behind the curtain of winter cloud and rain, a monolithic shadow towered over all else. It was the Citadel—the great tower-fortress that stood at the heart of the city. At its peak sat the Silver Throne, now empty since the last of the emperors was gone and the throne's heir lost nearly two centuries ago. The holy line of the emperors may be no more, but as long as the Citadel stood and the Lord Marshal remained prefect of the realm, a flame still flickered against the dark. And, as long as the Inquisition still held office, that flame would cast out any evil from the shadows.

Blackwood looked out at the moat of people between himself and the station and adjusted his grip on the handle of his leather letter bag. With the other, he drew the sigil of the Inquisition from beneath his coat and moved it so it hung neatly at the centre of his chest. The red-gold of the double cross hung heavily from the band of black beads around his neck. It was a sanctified symbol. A grim symbol.

Blackwood stepped from off the street corner and strode into the mass of people. The cold wind blew again, pulling his coat out behind him. His hat sat firmly on his head, its wide brim casting a dark shadow over his face. As he made his way to the arched entrance of the station, the crowd parted before him and no one dared to look him in the eye. He could feel their hurried glances gaze at the double-cross hanging from his neck before they scurried out of his way. His path through the crowd took him past the cluster of priests before the angel statue. The people continued to part before the inquisitor as he advanced. The holy men paused as they watched the dark figure from the Citadel stalk through the crowd like he was a lion moving through a trapped flock of sheep. For a moment, the loud voices of the crimson preachers stuttered and fell to nothing more than a murmur. The religious fervour faltered in their eyes. Blackwood offered them no regard. It was an insult to not acknowledge the men of the Church, but Blackwood was no ordinary man and the laws that governed them did not apply to him. The priests were in the wrong city too. They were in the capital, and that was under the Lord Marshal's rule. If he so wished, Blackwood could have them escorted onto a train heading back to the Bishop King's city. Worse still, he could have them thrown into a cell beneath the Citadel. The holy men knew this, and despite the anger writhing beneath their pious expressions, they did nothing to reprimand the inquisitor's lack of respect. As soon as they fell to his rear, the holy men picked up their calls of holiness again, praising and preaching to their gathering congregation with a new enthusiasm— undoubtedly to spite the inquisitor. *Dogs.* The word was clean and harsh in the forefront of Blackwood's mind as he discarded their presence from his thoughts. He moved swiftly, his long legs consuming the paved ground beneath him in deliberate strides. Blackwood's passage through the mass left a clear wake behind him and, in a matter of moments, he walked beneath one of the great arched entrances to the train station and left the cold stink and chaos behind.

Inside, a wide concourse ran from north to south and, like the limbs of a grotesque spider, a dozen metal staircases led down to platforms below. Blackwood looked up at the vast window occupying the upper reaches of the northern end of the concourse. On better days, the sunlight would pour through the great panes of glass and wash the terminal with brightness, but now there was just the gloom of the approaching the winter. In the distance, dark plumes of industry smoke rose into the sky, smudging the grey clouds like running trails of charcoal. Blackwood marched on. He had a train to catch. *Platform seven*, his ticket said. The terminal was a grand jewel of the new age. Giant statues carved from black marble—monuments to the Citadel's alchemists, the masterminds behind the great train station—

lined either side of the wide concourse. Each looming alchemist cradled a glass orb in their marble palms and, within each orb, the sickly green glow of gaslight burned. Overhead, the high vaulted ceiling of the dome presided with its great panelled paintings. From above, depictions of the emperors—Dominique and Pangallion—looked down at the countless people hurrying along the concourse. The latter carried the gift of illumination in his open hands, and the former bore freedom at the tip of a sword. Columns of polished grey stone ran along the edge of the terminal's circular interior, rising from the ground to meet the descent of the dome, thereby forming a wondrous gallery. Blackwood found the nature of the terminal a contradiction. Its exterior was adorned with the religious icons of the Church, whilst inside it seemed like a temple to the emperors and their alchemists. The world was a contradiction now, the Inquisitor thought.

He navigated his way across the concourse. Still, people avoided him and averted their eyes as he approached. Most were too busy scurrying along to catch their train, whilst others kept to themselves and lingered along the edge of the wide walkway. The terminal was filled with the voices of hundreds of people. The din rose to the domed ceiling in a great murmur that sounded like the ceaseless rains that were yet to come. A shrill whistle from a train erupted from a platform below, shattering the incessant human chatter like a bolt of lightening. Making his way along the concourse, Blackwood counted the numbered staircases that led to their respective platforms. Another train whistle screamed over the din of the station and a ragged figure burst from the crowd ahead of Blackwood. It was one of the forsaken souls of the Unclean Quarter, a worn, elderly man dressed in tattered rags that barely seemed to hold onto his bony shoulders. A sunken face, scarred with the marks of a life lived too long, caught the inquisitor's eye. Unlike the others, the beggar met Blackwood's stare and held it. The wretch's stare was empty, except for the faint flicker of hope that still lingered in the corners of his eyes. Slowly, the beggar stretched out his arms, palms turned to the ceiling like shallow cups, and with a gentle nod asked the inquisitor for charity.

Blackwood admired the man's tenacity. There were few who could stand before an inquisitor and hold themselves together. Whatever composure the beggar still possessed, it was more than Blackwood had seen from men who had proclaimed their courage to face an inquisitor. Blackwood would give the man a handful of coppers if it were up to him, if he were allowed to entertain the inkling of respect for the beggar that now itched in his heart, but the code which governed the Inquisition prevented him from doing so. Instead, he acknowledged the man with a simple nod.

"Look over there," a voice called out from somewhere in the heavy traffic of the concourse. The unseen voice was loud and commanding, its words clearly heard over the raucous of the passing people. "Look at the Inquisitor," the voice bellowed out again. Blackwood looked away from the beggar and scanned the concourse, his dark eyes taking in the face of each passing stranger as he shifted his gaze from left to the right. Nearly at the other end of the concourse, on the edge of his right shoulder, Blackwood found a woman amongst the crowd who was undoubtedly the owner of the domineering voice. She stared at Blackwood with an intensity that was a mixture of excitement and anger. Bright blue eyes shone from a face framed by long grey hair. A thick line of black ash ran down the centre of the woman's forehead, and she wore a robe of a similarly ashen-coloured fabric. *Scarolen*, Blackwood thought. The woman was a rogue priestess broken free from the Church. A small group of people were gathered around the Scarolen and they too stared at Blackwood. Some collapsed immediately beneath the gaze of the inquisitor as his black eyes moved over them. Others, riled by the blasphemous words from the desolate preacher, stood their ground against Blackwood's attention. He could see the fear slowly creep over them as he turned to face the small group of disheveled listeners.

"See how the servants of the Citadel do nothing for the people of the city," the Scarolen cried out again. Her deep voice seemed to rally the spirits of this small congregation and they pulled together. Some nodded and continued to look at Blackwood, whilst others turned to listen to the fallen priestess's words. The Scarolen stretched out her arms, beckoning her listeners to come closer, and they did. The woman was beginning to draw attention to herself. Blackwood noticed others along the concourse shifting their eyes nervously between the Scarolen and himself. The beggar from the Unclean Quarter was gone too. He must have retreated back into the mingling mass of people. It was a rare sight to see someone challenge an inquisitor, let alone to see it done in such a public place for no other reason than to gather a larger audience, never mind the group of priests doing the Church's work outside the station. The woman was stuck between two different sets of wolves. *She is mad, or she's a heretic,* Blackwood thought. Either way, her life in the city would be short-lived if she continued with these public demonstrations.

The Scarolen directed a skeletal hand toward Blackwood and pointed a long finger at the double-cross on his chest. "They say peace has come. They who reside in the great black tower. They say the *Old Ways* are gone. Yet, the people still live under the shadow of fear." Her listeners nodded their heads and mumbled in appreciation of her words. "The emperors are gone. The Lord Marshal rules with a tyrant's hand and the Church has been pushed out of the city while the bishop calls himself a king." Despite the loud murmur of the busy station and the din that echoed like rainfall through the high dome, Blackwood could make out the slight percussion of applause from the heretic's audience. The Scarolen paused for a moment and stared at her congregation. Her eyes flashed dangerously and a thin line of perspiration broke on her upper lip. More people were beginning to gather around the woman, eager to hear what she had to say. She was treading a dangerous line. So were these people. Simply entertaining the words of a blasphemer was punishable. The rogue priestess gathered her ashen cloak around herself and cleared her throat. "How can there be peace when those who should be looking after the welfare of the people bicker for power? The Church has lost its way. Those crimson wolves seek only to build their own kingdom in this world. And the Citadel has shut its doors. The Lord Marshal looks only to build industry while you starve; while you linger in the dirt and wait for the fruits of peace to be delivered."

The Scarolen pointed her long finger at the double-cross on Blackwood's chest again, but her eyes remained focused on the people she addressed. Tears appeared to well up in the woman's eyes as the fervour of her speech overcame her. "And then there are the inquisitors, the dark butchers of the Citadel that walk amongst us but are not of us. They observe and wait, still looking for signs of the *Old Ways*. But they tell us the *Old Ways* are dead, do they not?" The Scarolen paused to let her question resonate with her audience. "More lies. The butchers still hold their watch because they know the *Old Ways* still linger. Look at the witch hunter. He only cares for the destruction of the fae. He doesn't care for any of you.

None of you matter to him. Stand in his way, and he'll put you down. I've seen it before, my fellow citizens."

Blackwood remained still but he could feel more eyes upon him. He could kill the woman where she stood and carry on with his business. Blackwood looked around from the shadow of his wide brim hat and caught the uneasy stares of those surrounding the Scarolen. *They know it too*, he thought. The heretic's little congregation was beginning to look unsettled. Nervous glances were being exchanged and those who had gathered along the concourse were beginning to leave, continuing on their way. There was no need to kill the heretic. Her own words were turning against her and the authority of the Citadel, although imperfect—and Blackwood knew of its flaws—could not be challenged, let alone be brought down by the likes of the Scarolen.

The congregation began to break apart as people realised the rogue preacher was leading them down a dangerous path. The Scarolen reached out with both her arms, helplessly beckoning her fair-weather followers to stay and listen. She pushed her voice and began to speak even louder. Tears fell down her face as she pleaded with them to stay. "Do not leave my fellow people. Stay and listen. Do not be frightened by their lies. Stay and listen." No-one listened. Everyone left. The small cluster of people that had stood attentively only a few minutes ago had quietly dissolved into the flowing traffic along the concourse. Desperation and anger twisted the Scarolen's face, turning her narrow features into a vulturous mask of hatred. She looked across the crowd, bearing her eyes into Blackwood as more tears streamed down her face. "Smirk Inquisitor," sneered the heretic. "Go into the darkness and pursue your fiends, but you will see. No victory awaits you there." A malevolence filled the woman's eyes. The tellings of a lunatic left her face and a prophetic shadow seemed to take its place. The Scarolen looked more like a messenger of doom than a destitute heretic. "The Church is hollow and the Citadel will break, witch hunter. The darkness you hunt will soon unfurl its tattered wings and fill the sky. Then what will you and your ilk do? Burn the innocent again? Take to the fields and exterminate like you did before? There is no peace in this world. There is no light. There is only our doom."

Blackwood turned from the heretic and walked into the swarming crowd along the concourse. He'd heard enough from the doomsday prophet. On any other occasion he would take care of the heretic and cast judgement upon her right where she stood, issuing orders to have her escorted to the Citadel's prison. *The woman would never see another sun rise*. Fortune blessed the fallen priest though. Blackwood already had his own business to attend to. The hinterlands awaited him and there was only a single train per day. If he were to deal with the heretic he'd surely miss it. As he carried on his way, the crying voice of the woman followed him, slowly diminishing before being swallowed by the cacophony of the terminal. The Scarolen would become someone else's problem. Despite the madness in the woman's words and her blasphemous inclinations, Blackwood could not help but turn her words over in his mind as he approached the platform. Overhead, hanging from a chain bound to a pole-arm, an oval sign indicated platform six. In the near distance Blackwood could see the sign for platform seven looming above the concourse. Playing on the fears of the people was not a new invention. It was one of the oldest ploys in man's handbook of schemes. For now, the Scarolen were nothing but a pest in Gotheim, a sect of priests who refused to follow the Bishop King and his Church when the exodus from the city occurred. They were fear-mongers and nothing more, but the Citadel was watching them, and if the time came when their meddling became threatening, the Scarolen would be dealt with in a swift manner and with the utmost ease. The leader of the Scarolen was still a mystery—undoubtedly a strategic decision—and their exact cause remained unannounced. All that was known of the rogue priests and priestesses was their gospel of doom and their willing acceptance of a coming apocalypse. *Nihilists and heretics*, Blackwood thought.

He approached the top of the stairs that led down to platform seven. A line of people already stood along the platform saying goodbyes or waiting their turn to board the stationary train. Engineers and train personnel walked up and down, inspecting the impressive machine. At the head of the platform, a group of uniformed officers, the train managers, stood closely together whilst they examined a set of charts between them. Blackwood descended the stairs, the heels of his boots clicking against the metal of each step. The doomsday priest's words irked him. *What did the Scarolen know about darkness?* The woman's words were spoken out of ignorance and perhaps madness, but she touched on a truth the Citadel kept sealed behind its great walls. There was still darkness in the world and it was the business of the Inquisition to hunt what lurked behind that veil. Blackwood reached the platform and walked towards the train, ignoring the stolen glances of people. The train managers paused briefly from their discussions, their intelligent eyes quickly taking in the double-cross hanging from his chest before returning their attention to the charts in their hands. The inquisitor regarded the people as he passed them by, and contemplated their naivety. As he had come to see it, the world was a giant moth. At first glance, it seemed unimpressive and ordinary. Upon the surface of its fluttering wings, the lives of the common folk created complex and delicate patterns as they lived from day to day, carrying on with their natural pursuits, navigating their way through the meander of existence. The acceptance of peace and their belief that the darkest days had passed were a perfect mimicry of how things had been before the Wars of Religion. The people wanted calm. They wanted ordinary lives. A century of strife and violence fostered the strongest appetite for the mundane. Yet, beneath the patterns of mimicry, on the underside of those delicate wings, resided the foul dust of an ancient evil and the fine veins that spread its poison. Blackwood had seen the face of that underbelly. He had seen what monsters lay in wait beneath the surface of the peaceful world. All around him the elderly, parents with their children and folk deeply wrapped in the clutches of their own youth busied themselves with their affairs, unaware that the darkness they chose to forget still lingered in the world. Deep within the secret chamber of his heart, Blackwood had come to believe the darkness would always be there. It was as intrinsic to the world's existence, as the world was to its. Good and evil. Light and darkness. These were the two ends of the scale that balanced all things. *How long had he spent on the side of darkness?* The question seemed to present itself to him more often. Perhaps it had to do with his age. *There is only so much one can spend in the company of darkness, before it leaves its touch on you.* Veronica had said that to him, all those years ago. He quickly pushed the memory of her and those thoughts from his mind. She didn't understand the nature of the darkness either. *Veronica. The Scarolen.* He looked up and down the platform. *These people.* How could they understand what they had never witnessed.

A whistle from the top of the platform drew everyone's attention away from what they were doing. A call from an engineer on the other end signalled the last preparations for the train's departure. People hurried. Blackwood watched as a father shepherded his children into one of the train cars. A pair of lovers hurriedly concluded their farewell. Blackwood paused to look at the two youths for a moment. The tenderness and innocence shared between them seemed alien to him. He turned and made his way to the entrance of the train car. Large clouds of white steam began to drift down the platform as the train crew began to prepare the locomotive. Blackwood took hold of the railing and mounted the first step into the car. He glanced over his shoulder one more time and looked at the couple as they lingered in each other's arms. There was light between them. There was love. He examined them with his dark, brooding eyes. The young man cradled his lover's gentle face and she rested her gloved hands gently on his hips. There was a degree of decorum between them, Blackwood observed. They resisted the urge to smother each other, to behave inappropriately. These were the signs of high society. Blackwood noticed the happiness that shone in their eyes and lightened their faces. Compared to his dark eyes and hard face, they seemed bright and glorious. Blackwood relished their youth, for where he was going there would be no brightness or happiness. The borderlands awaited him and he would only find darkness and fear there.

2

THE CASE OF MARY SHAW

The train rocked from side to side as it sped through the countryside. Its engine whistled loudly, and the piston rods furiously turned the driving wheels forward. Long plumes of steam, like great white manes, drifted out against the grey skies overhead. The crew toiled in the driving cab. The stoker shovelled coal into the firebox and the engineer tapped at a series of gauges over the control levers. There was nothing to do to keep the cold weather out of the partially covered cab but to keep busy. The grey weather seemed unending, stretching from one horizon to the next, and the rain had not let up since the train departed from the main terminal station in Gotheim. The flatlands surrounding the city began to give-away to the rolling hills of the hinterlands—a green country-side pock-marked with scattered copses of trees—but behind the grey curtain of rain and gloom of the blanketing weather it now seemed a menacing landscape. The railway line snaked through the growing hills, crossing over bridged rivers and moving further away from the great city.

Blackwood sat quietly in a car near the end of the train, staring at the gloomy landscape as it passed by. Weeping trees upon the hilltops reminded him of the gargoyles that kept guard over the cathedrals of Gotheim—these standing watch over the flooded fields and grim wilderness. Rain splattered against the window. The reflection of a boy in the pane of glass caught his attention. For a moment, Blackwood watched the child stare at him via the reflection in the window. Beside the boy sat his mother. She too gaped at him. Slowly enough to give the boy and his mother the opportunity to break their stares, Blackwood turned his attention from the passing countryside and looked at them. As his eyes settled on them, they quickly diverted their gaze. The mother put her arm around her son, pushed his head to face the front of the train and looked down at her lap. Blackwood continued to stare at them. He studied first the child, and then the mother, and saw nothing unusual about them.

Blackwood was accustomed to having the eyes of the public on him; wherever he went people would stare with a mixture of awe and fear. He was an Inquisitor of the Citadel after all. For many, to see one of his order was still a novelty.

The weight of legend had much to do with that. Tales of the inquisitors' exploits during the *Wars of Religions* had shrouded them in mystery. Most of these stories had passed into the realm of myth, and to see an inquisitor in the flesh only added a hint of reality to the legends. *Those had been different times*, Blackwood thought. During the war, the inquisitors had been the elite honour guard of the emperor, the armoured legions of the Baldirim, which stood as the tip of the Citadel's spear against the *Old Ways*. It was a time of peace now, and the need for such warriors no longer existed. The wars had been over for nearly two centuries and the old enemy - the *fae* - had been eradicated. Yet, the wounds of that time had still not truly mended, and those who still remembered the horrors of the wars also recalled the grim shadow cast by the Inquisition. The older generations still remembered the purges, those ruthless hunts for the *fae-kind* which devastated not only the enemy population but that of the innocent too. The purges had been dark times, and the inquisitors had been at the heart of those nightmarish decades.

Peace reigned now, but the *Old Ways* still lingered, and the Council of the Suprema still hungered after its complete annihilation. The inquisitors were witch hunters and monster slayers now, men tasked with hunting down what remained of the *fae*. This was their duty to the Silver Throne.

Blackwood supposed the presence of an inquisitor reminded people that such creatures still existed, not just in the imagination of children, or in the nightmares of those who had once crossed paths with such demons.

There was something else though. No one was safe from an inquisitor's suspicion. The time of the *fae* was passing from the world. During the wars and purges, the true-born *fae* had been destroyed, and the felling of the great tree *Melendle* had been the final death knoll to what influence the *Old Ways* still held on the land. When the last branches of that ancient tree burned to ashes, the *Wars of Religions* ended. The last of the true-born were gone, faded from the world, but the half-born, those born from *fae* and human parents, still remained, and, as long as they still existed, the *Old Ways* would never truly disappear. There were the *inherent* too, human folk who gained gifts from the *Old Ways* at their coming of age. The *Old Ways* was a stubborn weed, and it still managed to maintain a hold on a world that wished to move on.

Blackwood looked at the woman and child again and found no sign of *fae* in them. There were no physical characteristics which would give them away. No pointed ears. No oddly coloured eyes. If either one of them were an *inherent*, there would be no way for him to tell, unless he pulled the black coin from his pocket and decided to do some true investigation. Yet that would only cause unnecessary commotion on the train and lead to a number of consequences he didn't have the energy to deal with. If the black coin was to draw something out the mother or the child, then Blackwood would be in his full right to pass judgement on them. But if there was nothing, he would find himself responsible for an upset and terrified mother and a petrified child, never mind the rest of the train's occupants if word spread that there was an inquisitor casting his black coin in search of *fae-kind*. Besides, he was on his way to Westgrave to investigate the case of Mary Shaw.

Blackwood pulled a time-piece from his coat pocket and clicked it open. It was nearing midday. The train would only reach Westgrave by nightfall. He closed the watch and tucked it back in his coat. He opened the letter bag on the chair next to him and, from one of its compartments, he pulled out a leather envelope. Pressed into its surface was the seal of the Citadel, the double-armed cross. He ran his fingers over the fine lines of the seal before unfurling the band that kept it closed. Inside was a collection of letters received from his apprentice who had been in Westgrave for a few weeks already, gathering information about the small town and Mary Shaw. Blackwood had already begun to piece the case together from what he had read in Fee's reports, but the last letter he had received had spurred him into action and he headed to Westgrave himself.

It was still rare for an inquisitor to travel to an outlying village like Westgrave, even if it was to investigate the occurrences of the *Old Ways*. Most cases occurred in densely populated areas like towns where larger sects of heretics could be found. In most outcomes of these investigations, the perpetrators were revealed to be nothing more than charlatans, racketeers on the prowl for easy coin from would-be believers or the curious wealthy. Nevertheless, tales of small towns being plagued by strange occurrences were on the rise and rumours were beginning to spread through the countryside.

Over the last few months Fee had been travelling from village to village, chasing rumours of witchcraft and druidism and looking for any truth behind the whispers of strange creatures wandering the wilds of the borderlands, preying on vulnerable travellers. Superstitions seemed to be returning and the echoes of the *Old Ways* continued to stir chaos amongst the more susceptible communities of village-folk. Of all the rumours and whispers chased, the case of Mary Shaw was the only one Fee stressed as requiring his attention. Of course, back in Gotheim, he had given his initial attention to the reports, as any thorough inquisitor would, but it was the latest developments which truly piqued his interest.

Blackwood had read Fee's last report several times since receiving it, and for some reason, he could not help but feel a growing shadow in the back of his mind. Perhaps the *Old Ways* were really at work in Westgrave.

Blackwood paged through the collection of reports, until he found the first letter from Fee that mentioned Mary Shaw. It was dated Marun 31, 896 …

Master Blackwood,

.   .   .

I find myself in the village of Westgrave, a humble settlement in the heart of the eastern hinterlands. Not much can be said of this place, except that it is what you would expect. The village is nothing more than a stop on the way to other parts of the world. If not for its location along the great coastal road running from Hellendel to Gotheim, I doubt this village would even exist. Nevertheless, here I find myself. The rain is unceasing in the hinterlands, and the weather creeping in from the north carries the cold of the sea. I would not wish to stay here out of my own accord, but a strange tale worthy of investigation has brought me here.

To explain why I find myself in Westgrave, I need to recall an encounter from a few nights past whilst travelling along the great coast road. Although I often cease my journeying with the setting sun, on this occasion a restlessness had found a home within me, and I chose to continue with my travels rather than take rest. Making my way west, I came to a crossing, where a lesser country road intersected the great highway. It was here that a lone rider approached from the country road and asked to join my company, for he was heading in the same direction. Although I was restless, I had no desire for company, but before I declined the man's company I remembered your teaching—"What truths are shared as tales between strangers on the road". With your words in mind, I acquiesced to the stranger's request.

If I were to speak of the man's character, less honourable things could be said. To say the least, the man had a slanderous tongue for the Citadel, and apart from his foul mouth, the stranger was odd. By the sound of his voice I am sure he was of the parts—I assumed a travelling hand, looking for work, or just a wanderer of familiar lands. Regardless of his circumstance, the man was strange, perhaps a symptom of his loneliness. I did little to open the man up to me; it seemed my presence was the only nudge he needed to speak freely. I remained amiable to the man's stories, agreeing where I should and nodding when appropriate, and it did not take long before the man exhausted all news about himself. It was then that he reverted to tales fitting our scenario—rumours and ghost stories for a dark night on the road. All of his tales I had heard before, as would you. It seems that country folk, never mind their origin, all scoop their folklore from the same well. I paid little interest to these, and my disinterest only spurred the man on. Desperate to capture my attention, he then proceeded to tell me a tale, not from the well of age-old folklore, but that seemed to be borne from the very land we travelled through.

He told me of Westgrave and the tale of the girl who had been taken by death and yet not died. At night, it was said, she walked the streets of the town, her eyes as white as the moon, and always to the woods she wandered. To talk to the lady of the woods, this man asserted—although I don't believe this to be part of the rumours from Westgrave. Witchcraft, he claimed. According to what he had heard, the girl also spoke to the dead, her young voice recalling times long before any living person's memory. The man continued with his tale and I listened carefully, still maintaining my appearance of disinterest.

For your benefit Master Blackwood, as I find myself

dawdling in my report to you, I will get to the point. The man's tale was of local origin. Yes, there are similarities to be found with the common tales of bewitchings, but I felt that this was a rumour requiring further investigation. And, considering the long list of rumours I have already investigated these past months, there could be no harm in looking into another. After all, this is my task here in these banal hinterlands—to be your eyes and ears.

May this find you in good health.

Your servant,
  Fee.

Blackwood placed the letter back into the leather enveloped and perused the remainder of Fee's updates. According to his apprentice's reports, the village of Westgrave was a quiet settlement, nothing more than a thoroughfare to Stone Harbour. It consisted mostly of merchant stores, established to trade with those heading to the coast, and an inn for those weary of the road. The inn, the largest building in the village, had been built by a family—the Shaws. Originally from Gotheim, they had moved to the village some years ago. The inn had flourished as a layover for tradesmen, merchants and travellers seeking voyage by sea. By Fee's account, the Shaws had several children and the family appeared to be well-respected in the community. Blackwood glanced over the penultimate letter received from his apprentice, seeking the most pertinent information—the recorded date in its upper corner marked the day 5 Arun, 896...

. . .

*It has been several days since arriving in Westgrave and I
have taken on the guise of a traveller heading to Stone
Harbour. There is no other lodging in this dreary town but the
inn itself, which has suited my needs quite nicely without
arousing suspicion from the locals, even more so, the Shaw
family. So far, parts of the stranger's tale have proven true.
The girl—Mary be her name—has taken ill, or, more accu-
rately, she has fallen into the grips of an unnatural slumber.
According to the residents of the village, she has yet to stir
from this sleep, not since the night she walked into the
common room of the inn, as if in the grips of some trance,
and proceeded to speak words no one could understand.*

*Of what I've managed to overhear from local murmurings
around the common room, the girl began to act strangely
before succumbing to whatever ailment now possesses her.
According to the children of the village, the days before Mary
Shaw fell into the grip of her unnatural slumber, she began to
speak of a lady in the woods. A lonesome woman who spied
on the village from the trees and envied their parents for
having the gift of children.*

*These are strange tales, but I have yet to see any evidence
with my own eyes that would separate this from backwater
fearmongering. I shall remain here for a few more days to see
what I can uncover. Perhaps I may come...*

The inquisitor folded the report in half before finishing the final sentences on the page and looked out the window of the train as he blindly added the letter to the envelope. The light was already beginning to fail, due no doubt to the weather. The rain renewed itself against the windowpane, blurring the landscape into a swampy blend of darkening colours. The last time he had looked at these early reports was some time ago, and it was good to refresh his memory. It was only wise to arrive in Westgrave as fully abreast of the situation as he could be. Fee's reports were thorough. The boy had taken to his training with ease and his keen mind and attentiveness to detail leant him well to this kind of work. It was one of the reasons he had dispatched the boy to the hinterlands. The better years of his manhood were behind him. He was far from incapable of carrying himself in situations requiring the special skills of an inquisitor or of spending time on the road. After all, he had spent most of his life in the saddle and, if luck allowed it, in strange beds at night. But now he was beyond that life. Besides, he had an apprentice now and it was Fee's rite of passage to venture as his outrider.

The inquisitor turned his attention back to the paper in his hand—the last letter to be received from Fee and the report that had prompted him to leave the Citadel with all haste. If his suspicions proved to be true, then Fee and the village of Westgrave were in dire peril. The letter in his hand carried the date of two days past—14 Arun, 896—and had arrived at the Citadel by black messenger bird. The black bird, only used for calamitous news, had been the first sign of what he would find in the letter. Blackwood opened the final report and re-read each line, careful to absorb each detail his apprentice had documented.

Master Blackwood,

. . .

Please excuse the terrible condition of my handwriting, but I write this letter with a trembling hand, and even though I have tried to steady it, I fear it still shakes from what I have witnessed.

Days have passed at a tedious pace in Westgrave, with no mentionable developments in the case of Mary Shaw. I had almost given up and discarded the whispers of the country folk as mere conjecture and rumour. So much so that I made to my room to pack my belongings—strange to think how nearly this letter would have been of a different nature had the following events not occurs—events that have chilled me to my bones.

As I was saying, I made my way from the common room to my lodging situated on the upper level of the floor. For your reference, this so happens to be the same floor upon which the Shaw family have kept their daughter. The night was deep into its reign as I came onto the landing at the head of the staircase, and it was there that I saw the girl— Mary Shaw— at the end of the passageway. She stood as still as a statue and, although the light was poor, I could see she was as bare as the day she was born. I quickly concealed myself against the wall of the landing, not wishing to startle the girl as she seemed out of sorts. For my own sake, I also could not stand to embarrass the girl by hovering upon the landing. And, thank the light of the emperor, that I had done so. Not moments after I pressed myself against the wall, Mary began to approach the landing. She walked past me with a slow gait, and I know that, had she been in control of her own senses, she would have seen me, for my place of hiding could barely be called that. The girl passed by, and as she did, I caught a glimpse of her eyes. They were as white as snow, as if milk had been poured into them. If she had looked at me in that moment, I would have been overcome with fear; the paralysing kind that leaves a man helpless in the face of fear. A coward's fear. I'm not proud of that but fear itself followed in the girl's wake. So did death. As she passed by, the smell of the open grave came behind her. The smell of deep black earth and decay filled the passageway. I have encountered that stink before in the dens of the resurrectionists in the city. I can still smell the dank rot, even now as I write these words. The girl went down to the common room and, gathering my wits, I pursued her with caution. The night was late, but the common room still held a few stragglers; those unwanting of the comforts of their own homes.

What I saw next I know will never leave me, for it will always remind me of what waits for me in the darkness beyond the light of the emperor. I would never withhold information from you Master Blackwood, but I cannot recall the words the girl spoke. However, I swear on my own fate that Mary Shaw spoke the fae-tongue in the common room. Whether it be possession or witchcraft, it was not Mary Shaw who addressed those who remained in that place. Even stranger still, once the girl's foul monologue ceased, she proceeded to exit the inn— naked as a newborn—and walk up the main street toward the woods that lie at the edge of town. Not even her father possessed the courage to follow his child out into the darkness. Yet, and I hope this makes you proud to read, as my duty demanded, I trailed the girl from a safe distance and watched as she stood at the edge of the trees, seemingly unperturbed by the awful weather which seems to haunt this place. For what seemed like an eternity, Mary Shaw held her ground before the dark boughs of the woods and resumed her slurring speech in what I still claim to be the fae-tongue. At long last, the girl turned and made her way back to the inn, the trail of death following closely behind her, that smell as strong in the falling rain as it was in the confines of the passageway.

These events I swear to, and before the court of the Suprema I would hold testament. With these words, I pray to summon you to Westgrave, for all means of darkness are at work here, and I fear for the fate of Mary Shaw…

Fae'lar Essenta Per'culum.

Your servant,
    Fee.

Blackwood lingered on those three words—*Fae'lar Essenta Per'culum*—the formal inquisitorial declaration of the *Old Ways*. What Fee said must be true. He did not doubt his apprentice's claims, especially not if the declaration had been used. From the outset of training, the weight of that declaration was made clear. Once made, it could not be undone. Once declared, an inquisitor was bound by law to investigate, and once an inquisitor set out to uncover the truth, resolution could only be achieved with the damnation of the guilty, regardless if the true presence of the *Old Ways* was at work. How many innocents had been put to death beneath the iron fist of those three words? The question had seemed to gather more weight in Blackwood's mind as he gained in his years, but the same answer always set him at ease in the pursuit of his duty. *How many innocents had been saved by those three words.*

The inquisitor looked out at the grim countryside again and pondered on such things. Whatever was happening in Westgrave, he would uncover it. *Punishment or damnation.* The scale of these two outcomes shifted from side to side in his mind as he pieced together the facts laid out by his apprentice. The sentence his hand would cast remained unseen, but one thing was certain as the train snaked through the countryside to the rhythm of its steam engine: each passing moment brought him close to Westgrave; each rotation of the wheels brought Mary Shaw closer to her fate.

3

WESTGRAVE

The village appeared through the gloom like a headland along a foggy coast. The station emerged first as the train slowed its approach on the railway line. Lamps burned dimly in the failing light, phantasmal will-o'-the-wisps hovering in the thickening shroud, beckoning the train to come to a halt before the deserted platform. The rain had ceased some time ago and given way to a blanketing fog. Blackwood peered out of the window and watched as the village loomed silently beyond the station. Curved rooftops rose and fell in the sea of fog, like the humps of one of those sea creatures heard in sailors' tales. The dark doors of each home and building were shut tight against the weather and the village looked black and unwelcoming. The ghostly atmosphere was dispelled by the high pitched whistle of the train and, with a jolt, the train came to a stop alongside the sole platform outside of Westgrave.

No one in Blackwood's car made to gather their belongings and leave the train. The inquisitor was the only one. His movement attracted the attention of the other passengers. Putting the remaining letters into the leather envelope and then placing that into the letter bag, Blackwood folded his coat over his arm and moved to the door of the car. He could feel the eyes of every passenger follow his departure. Although he had made no open display of his position, the double-cross hanging from his neck was enough for people to know who, and what, he was. There were a few hushed whispers as he stood up—no doubt once he had left the train, the rumour mill would begin amongst the passengers remaining on the train.

Someone would ask, "What is he doing in Westgrave?"

Another would query, "Have you heard anything strange about Westgrave?"

"It was only a matter of time before the superstitions of these backward country folk got them in trouble with the Citadel. I heard that some of these little villages still enlist the help of medicine men."

And so the whispers and hushed debates would continue until Westgrave became a distant memory along the train's winding route. Blackwood had heard all the conjecture before —and it was always the same. As he reached the door to exit the car, Blackwood caught the eyes of the little boy staring at him again. The child looked at him with an incredulous awe, as if the inquisitor had walked out of a bedtime story. It was obviously the first time the child had seen an inquisitor. The boy's mother stared at him too, but her eyes were filled with fear, and it appeared as if she were on the edge of tears. It was not the first time she had seen an inquisitor. He could see in her trembling tears the knowledge of an inquisitor's business, and he wondered on what side of the fence she stood. Again the thought struck him: *How many innocents had been put to death by the declaration of Fae'lar Essenta Per'culum?* And, as always, his mind answered, *How many innocents had been saved by those three words?*

The train's siren call whistled through the silence cast by the fog as it rattled into its slow forward motion and pulled away from the station.

Blackwood stood alone on the platform, his dark figure a stark imposition against the thick fog that swirled about him. The air was thick and damp, and he could feel the cold touch of the misty air upon his face. He fastened his coat, closed to the top button beneath his chin and looked to either side. A line of lamps ran from one end of the platform to the next, the orbs of light at the head of each disappearing into the distance, consumed by the gloom. The inquisitor sucked on his teeth with a grimace and made his way off of the platform. *Fee, where are you?* He had expected his apprentice to be waiting for him when he arrived and yet there was no sign of him. Blackwood followed the lamps into the darkness, each one disappearing behind him as another revealed itself on the path ahead. The hollow clicks of his boot heels against the cobbled path were the only sounds in the white shroud. Nothing else stirred, not even the shadows that come with the night crawled from their lairs. The fog, almost suffocating in its thickness, was all consuming. Blackwood grabbed the collar of his coat in a fist and tightened it around his neck to keep out the chill. In the absence of his apprentice he pushed on, taking the cobbled pathway beneath his feet as the only guidance that he was walking in the right direction. There were no discernible landmarks, and beside his own footfalls, no sounds to orientate himself, just the line of lamps leading the way through the gloom. He began to count the distance between each ghostly pool of light. *One… Two… Three…* On each count of seven, a new lamp appeared in the distance. He repeated the count several times, and only on the ninth count did a shift beneath the lamp ahead catch his eye. He may be considered aged by his younger compatriots, but his eyes were still sharper than any other. He paused for a moment. Beyond the lamp ahead came the dim glow of another. The strange light floated in the fog, swaying gently from side to side, like a firefly in the belly of the night. Blackwood turned his feet, positioned himself, and waited. He had not received another report from Fee, and who knew what evils may have occurred in the time between the last letter and his arrival. *Especially if the Old Ways were at work here.* With one hand he held the letter bag before him like a shield, and with the other, he reached behind his back and took hold of the smooth handle beneath his coat. He watched as the light grew closer, slowly brightening through the gauzy fog. If whatever approached chose to be his enemy, he would be ready. His fingers adjusted themselves along the handle of the weapon concealed beneath his coat. The moments stretched on as he watched the light approach. But it was no enemy that broke the curtain of fog before him. At first, a lantern appeared out of the murk, then the hand and arm that carried it. A moment later, Fee emerged from the fog, his face drawn and pale in the umbra of the lantern's light. Blackwood released his grip on the handle and relaxed his stance. Ordinarily, he would have felt foolish for his cautious behaviour, but he had lived through too many close encounters to not take guard against the unknown.

Fee lifted the lantern up above his shoulder, thereby broadening the pool of light that it cast. The apprentice's appearance was both startling and a source of pride for the inquisitor. It had only been a few months since Blackwood sent Fee from the Citadel, but the change in the young man was apparent. His boyish looks—the plumpness of a noble-man's son and the immaculately kept hair of a gentleman—

were gone, and, in their place, was the worn look of one who now called the road his home. Fee's cheeks had sunken and his jawline protruded with definition, revealing the first features that would mark the face of the man he was set to become. His hair was combed for the most part, but was much longer than Blackwood remembered, and a fine shadow of beard covered his cheeks. He no longer looked like the boy Blackwood had taken in as his apprentice. The first signs of the life he had chosen were beginning to take hold, and Blackwood could not help but take comfort in it. *There's an inquisitor in you yet, boy.*

"Master Blackwood," whispered Fee, his voice slightly out of breath.

Against the surrounding murk the lantern's light was harsh. With the back of a gloved hand, Blackwood gently pushed the lantern away from his face. "Good evening, Fee." His voice was flat and rough. "I thought I could expect you at the station."

"Apologies". Fee adjusted his grip on the handle of the lantern, his cheeks reddening slightly.

Yet in many ways still a boy, Blackwood mused.

"Slipping out of the inn unseen proved more difficult than I assumed," the apprentice continued. "I eventually made my way through the kitchen and out the back door, just in …"

Blackwood stopped him with a raised hand. "Why are you skulking about?" the inquisitor asked. There was a hint of incredulity in his words.

"Since the last occurrence, the one covered in my last report, the inn has become a sort of safe haven for the village folk."

"So there have been no other occurrences since?" Blackwood questioned.

Fee shook his head. "No, not since that night. But strange

things have been taking place, and there have been other developments."

Blackwood raised an eyebrow. "Other developments?"

Fee looked about as if to check the fog for any wandering ears. "Yes, but I think that would be better spoken about in the comfort of the inn. To your first question though, the people of Westgrave are adhering to an unspoken curfew. They're afraid of what may be lurking under the cover of darkness, especially close to the edge of the town where the woods begin. Even in the daylight the village folk keep away from the tree line. Not to say that they would keep me against my free will, but I choose to avoid any course of action that may lead to an altercation. The people are terrified, and there are others I believe who are gathering at the inn for the chance to witness another one of Mary Shaw's unnatural spells."

"Well, I think they're all in for a surprise when we come through the front door," Blackwood stated, matter-of-factly.

Fee forced a grin. "Perhaps. Unless they've already noticed my absence and have jumped to the conclusion that I've been abducted by a hobgoblin."

The apprentice's attempt at a joke did little to stir humour in the inquisitor. As if not hearing Fee's last words, Blackwood asked the question that had been scratching at him since reading the apprentice's last letter. "You signed your last report to me with the declaration of malfeasance. I do not doubt your conviction, but still I must ask, for even now we have passed the point of return. Do you still stand by it?"

Fee met the inquisitor's hardened eyes and did not look away when he answered. "I do."

"Then we have a lot to discuss."

Fee nodded. He did not bother looking for his master's luggage. Inquisitors never travelled with much for they never intended to stay in one place for long. Their business simply does not allow for it. With the lantern clutched in the grip of his hand, he pointed in the direction from where he came. "Shall we?"

"Lead the way, young sir."

Blackwood followed Fee through the fog. The two men walked in silence. The night was growing old and the air was gathering the cold about itself. After walking some distance through the chill, a building appeared through the drifting veil of weather. The inn was a two-story stone building with a tiled roof. Large windows along the ground floor glowed with warm light and the shadows of people criss-crossing inside. Smaller windows on the upper floor—rooms, Blackwood assumed—were mostly dark, although some hinted at the dim flicker of a candle.

Fee walked up the few stairs leading onto the deck and turned to face the inquisitor. "Welcome to *The Candle and Cask*, Master Blackwood," he announced in a hushed voice. He lifted the latch of the lantern casing and blew out the flame. The pool of light was swallowed by darkness and the two men were engulfed by the night. Fee opened the door to the inn and a large square of light spilled out onto the deck.

Blackwood paused for a moment before striding into *The Candle and Cask*.

4

DARK OMENS

Whatever activity was happening inside *The Candle and Cask* ceased upon the entry of the inquisitor and his apprentice. Men, halfway between standing and sitting, remained frozen in their awkward configurations, their eyes locked on the two men. Others huddled around tables or standing beside the bar now faced the entrance to the inn. Behind the counter stood the innkeeper. He was a scrawny, bird-like man. In one hand he held a mug and, in the other, a cleaning cloth. Blackwood peered around the room, taking in each element in a matter of moments. The walls were covered with large paintings of the surrounding areas. Some depicted twisted woodlands, obvious portrayals of the woods which lay beyond the town boundary, whilst others showed landscapes of bog-like pits filled with stricken trees. If these were the semblances of the area, then Westgrave truly was a solemn and miserable place. Situated between the paintings were animal trophies. A wide array of stags, their horns casting thorny shadows against the walls, looked down at the common room with lifeless, black eyes. Mounted upon the shelves were taxidermies of birds and foxes, their skins and feathers beginning to take on a grey film of deterioration. At the centre of the ceiling a great wooden chandelier, no doubt carved from the trees of the local woods, hung from a thick chain—the countless candles upon it casting an inadequate light for the size of the room. Against the far wall a wide hearth hosted a roaring fire, its dancing flames making up for what the chandelier failed to provide. Deep shadows gathered in the corners of the common room where the light from the fire could not reach. All considered, between the paintings and the collection of dead animals, *The Candle and Cask* was a macabre inn.

Blackwood undid his coat and walked across the common room. The eyes of the patrons—some seemed to be merchants, but mostly appeared to be local village-folk—followed the inquisitor's steps across the wooden floorboards. At the bar, he placed the letter bag at his feet and rested his hands palms down onto the countertop. He met the stares of those closest to him, their eyes jumping between his cold eyes and the mark of the Citadel hanging from the beaded necklace. Fee came to stand beside him. For an awkward moment all parties around the bar looked at each other with a tense apprehension—everyone but the inquisitor. He looked straight at the barman with an implacable stare that would make any man shiver. Unable to hold the inquisitor's glare, the barman glanced quickly toward the other village men standing at the bar, perhaps hoping for some kind of moral support. As if his plea was diseased, his compatriots looked away or searched the bottom of their glasses for something that wasn't there.

"I hadn't noticed your absence," the barman managed. There was barely a stammer, but his voice wavered.

Fee opened his mouth and a faint smile curled into the edges of his lips. It was the kind of smile that preluded a polite gentlemanly reply, but it was Blackwood who spoke, his voice hard and sharp as glass. "Mr. Shaw, I presume?"

The innkeeper froze at the mention of his name, and with evident reluctance, he turned to face Blackwood again. The inquisitor could feel the eyes of the other patrons upon him. From the corner of his eyes, he could see their faces turned toward him.

"Yes, I am he," the man managed.

"And who may you be, stranger?" barked a voice from the rear of the common room. Blackwood glanced over his shoulders, his dark eyes—almost black in the flickering fire-light—pin-pointing the speaker with unerring accuracy. The man was easily the largest in the room, with broad shoulders, thick arms and a jutting belly that looked more hard than soft. By the look of the men sitting at the table with him, the burly man had a strong pack of lackeys. The inquisitor buried his hand into the pocket of his trousers and pulled out a simple black coin. He turned and watched as realisation dawned on the face of the burly man and his henchman. First, their eyes fell on the silver pendant that marked him as an agent of the Citadel. The colour drew from their faces. The inquisitor then watched as the black coin in the palm of his hand drew their attention. At the sight of it, a wildfire of fear sparked in their eyes and a hushed gasp filled the room. The black coin was simple, a little larger than a regular coin, but it was the sigil pressed into its surface that caused the shock. Everyone's eyes were now fixed on the black token. Even Mr. Shaw leaned over the bar countertop to catch a glimpse of it. The coin was the true mark of an inquisitor. If the inquisitors were shrouded in dark rumour and speculation, then the black coin of their order was something of legend.

Blackwood presented the coin in his upturned palm, moving it from one side to the other so that everyone could see it. "I am Marcus Blackwood, of the Citadel. This token here marks my station and authority. Does anyone here challenge my sigil?"

The room was silent—and, with that single question, the inquisitor crushed any challenger to his presence. The burly man sunk back into his chair and his lackeys shied away like reprimanded dogs. Blackwood returned the coin to his trouser pocket and turned back to the bar. The uneasiness in the room was at the point of danger. The last thing Blackwood needed was resistance from the local people, even if his presence as an inquisitor sparked fear. He pointed at the bottle of whiskey on the counter and then held up two fingers. "We'll have two of that," he asked. The request was polite but there was no softness in his voice.

Whilst Mr. Shaw gathered two glasses from the back shelf, polished them with the cloth in his hand and then made to pour the servings of whiskey, Blackwood began to speak, or rather, he began to explain to Mr. Shaw and the small audience what was going to happen next, now that he was in Westgrave. The memory of the black coin still held them in his command, and they listened to his words.

"Let me address the state of affairs that has brought me to your village. My associate here, Mr. Fee, with whom you are familiar, has been observing the events in Westgrave and the condition of your daughter, Mary, under the authority of the Inquisition." At the mention of that last word, Mr. Shaw's hand trembled and a spout of whiskey spilled over the rim of one of the glasses and onto the counter.

Blackwood paused for a moment and allowed Mr. Shaw to steady his hand. "My presence here has been deemed worthy by the declaration of *Fae'lar Essenta Per'culum* and, as such, I exercise the rights of an inquisitor.

"Your daughter, Mary, has come under the influence of

some force unexplainable in the realms of men. I am here to investigate malfeasance and the presence of the *Old Ways*. To act against me is to act against the Citadel. To interfere is to stand against the will of the Silver Throne." Blackwood's voice filled every space in the hushed room and the air stirred as if his words possessed some power in themselves. His eyes, as black as the charred wood in the fireplace, imposed the power of the Inquisition and everyone in the room shrank before him. "Until my investigation is done, the village of Westgrave is under my custody. No one is beyond suspicion."

If the room was silent before, the blanket of quiet that presided over it now was oppressive. A blank state of comprehension had come over Mr. Shaw as he tried to reconcile the presence of the inquisitor with the fate of his daughter —who would be the focus of the inquisitor's scrutiny. Fear mingled with worry and tears began to arise over the lips of his eyelids. No one else stirred. Even the fire burning in the hearth seemed to have lost its comforting warmth. The shadows the far corners of the room deepened.

Blackwood tapped his finger on the counter. "For now, I would have those two whiskeys, and my associate and I will retire to a table by the fire. We have many things to discuss and wouldn't wish to be disturbed. Is that understood?"

Mr. Shaw pushed the glasses toward the inquisitor and his apprentice and managed a respectable reply. "Of course, Master Blackwood."

"And in the meantime, I would like a room to be prepared for myself here, at The Candle and Cask."

"Very well," stammered Mr. Shaw.

Blackwood gripped one of the glasses of whiskey and looked at the glow of the amber liquor. "When the time comes to examine your daughter, Mr. Shaw, I expect to receive your full cooperation. Is that understood?" The inquisitor's voice was sharp and cold now.

Mr. Shaw struggled against the turmoil of being a father. The fate of his daughter seemed doomed in every respect. An Inquisition would not show mercy, and yet he hoped the inquisitor may, even if Mary was a helpless victim in all of this. Those touched by the *Old Ways* never came out of it unscathed—especially with an inquisitor's involvement. The instinct to protect his daughter was overwhelming. On one hand, she would be taken by the *Old Ways* and, on the other, she would either be taken or punished by the Inquisition. Mary, his precious daughter, faced wolves at every turn. He met the stare of the inquisitor and did what any hopeless man would do: he played for time. "Of course," he answered again. This time the innkeeper spoke without expression.

The inquisitor and his apprentice chose a table in front of the hearth where the heat from the fire was comfortable and the pool of light was rich and held the shadows of the room at bay. They had dark things to discuss, and such matters were always better spoken of in the light. Blackwood sat back in his chair and stretched his one leg out toward the fire. The warmth of the flames began to creep through the sole of his boot and warm his foot. With his one hand he held the glass of whiskey. By the time they sat down, the room had mostly emptied. The burly man and his companions made their leave quickly after Blackwood walked past their table, and so had others, most probably to spread the word of an inquisitor in Westgrave. By morning, Blackwood's presence would be known by all in the village. Mr. Shaw remained behind the bar. A veil of complete despair hung over his face. The poor light from the chandelier offered him one grace, hiding the silent tears running down his cheeks.

"I thought you didn't drink while on the road," the apprentice, Fee, asked gently. Blackwood looked into the flames and watched the shapes dance from side to side. The flickering light did little to touch his dark eyes. "It puts the folk at ease to see one of us partaking in a ritual they're familiar with. It helps undo the shroud that follows inquisitors wherever we go," the inquisitor answered.

Fee looked over his master's shoulder at Mr. Shaw and what remained of the late evening patronage, and offered something of a laugh. "I'm sure it's working."

The laugh went unnoticed by the inquisitor, his attention fixed on the fire. The shadows cast by the flames exaggerated the lines in Blackwood's face, deepening the furrows across his forehead and the crow's feet around his eyes. Creases that spoke of weathering and trials beyond imagination ran down his cheeks. The creases seemed so deep in the light, one could mistake them for scars. Fee knew better though. Once, he had seen his master barechested—a sight rarer than the *Old Ways*, Fee liked to tell the other apprentices—and saw the myriad of scars that criss-crossed his chest and arms. Burn marks sprawled across his back—and some scars belied their age, still looking pink and only just healed. The thought of those wounds made Fee shiver. Despite the age of tales that lined the inquisitor's face, his eyes still shone with a fervour.

At last, Blackwood shifted his attention to his apprentice. The long journey from Gotheim had given him enough time to piece everything together from Fee's reports—all the pieces except for some, and he would know them before the night was through. "Tell me about the girl, Fee. This Mary Shaw. Tell me about the night you spoke of in your last report" His eyes were almost black, the flames in the hearth flickering in their darkness like watery coals.

Fee shifted in his seat, and Blackwood saw the boyish charm that once livened his apprentice's face fade away at his request. *Soon, there would be none of that boyhood wonder left. Soon, there will only be stone there.* Despite the warm glow of the fire, Fee's face seemed pale, as if the memory of that particular night caused him distress—and perhaps it did. The time would come when such occurrences would leave little effect on him. Blackwood knew this. *Only a matter of time.*

The apprentice glanced over Blackwood's shoulder before taking a long sip of his whiskey, and then he began to tell his master about Mary Shaw—about that particular night. "Well, as I mentioned in my report, the few days preceding that night had been extraordinarily quiet. I had seen the girl unconscious in her bed, and I had taken the time to speak to the village folk and walk along the tree line of the woods at the edge of Westgrave. From all accounts, Westgrave seemed untouched by any malevolence, the girl simply affected by an illness. As for the rumours of the lady in the wood, none of the village folk seemed to know what I was talking about, and the children would not speak to me. They appeared to be just that: rumours emerging out of local folklore or the imagination of children. On the night of the incident, I was sitting there," Fee pointed at a table across the room by the door, "and, considering all these elements, had decided Westgrave was just another false trail." Fee paused and took another sip of whiskey. Trepidation filled his eyes, but he continued. "As I mentioned in my letter, I made the decision to leave Westgrave, and, with that as my resolution, I made my way to my room upstairs to prepare for my departure. That was when I saw …"

. . .

... Mary Shaw in the darkness of the passageway. The girl
stood naked before the door to her room, her body beginning
to take on the shape of a woman, the light from the candles in
her room illuminating the curves and lines of her developing
breasts. Startled by the silhouette of the girl at the end of the
hall, Fee stood frozen for a moment. He could feel the embar-
rassment heat his cheeks as he looked at her bare form and
his heart froze in the cold grasp of fright. There was some-
thing wrong. Whatever it was, it was hidden from sight, but
he could sense it. His training at the Citadel focused on the
heightening of the senses to pick up such things, and although
he could not identify the unearthly aura which gnawed at
him, he could feel it permeate from the girl at the end of the
passage. Without a second thought, he moved to the side of
the landing and pressed his body against the wall. From his
hiding spot, Fee peered around the corner and looked at the
girl. She had begun to move down the passage, her bare feet
making no sound against the carpeted floor. The touch of
light from her bedroom left her body but, in the darkness of
the hall, her pale skin was clear to see. So were the ghostly
eyes that looked out from her expressionless face. Those eye,
white and unnatural, seemed to look beyond the hallway,
beyond the inn and into a world that the living could not see.
As Mary Shaw approached, Fee could feel the grip of fear
tighten its fingers around his heart. The sense that something
was terribly wrong grew stronger. It was aberrant. It was
malicious. A strange smell filled the passage ahead of Mary
Shaw's approach. The smell of an open grave. It conjured
thoughts of bone and curdled flesh, night crawlers and dank
soil. Fee stifled his reflex to throw up and lifted his handker-
chief to his nose. Mary seemed to glide past where he hid as if

she were being ushered by an unseen presence—his presence going unnoticed. The smell of rot deepened. Mary passed so close to where he was pressed against the wall that, if he so wished, Fee could stretch out his arm and put his hand on her shoulder. Paralysis had him completely though, and all he could do was watch the girl pass by him. As she did, Fee did not feel the presence of a young girl but something more ancient and conniving.

He watched as Mary made her way down the stairs to the common room. The screams from the patrons below, and what were bewildered outbursts from her father, broke the hold of fear over Fee. He scrambled down the stairs, following in the wake of the fetid stink and watched as Mary moved to the centre of the room with her arms stretched out to either side. Her long, black hair fell to the small of her back and it caught the light from the fire in the hearth. Patrons covered their noses in disgust, women looked for solace in the arms of their men, and the men stared with an awful mixture of abashment, appreciation and fear. Mary turned slowly, taking in each person with those lifeless marble-like eyes, as if she were acknowledging her court. Stretching beyond anatomical possibility, Mary's mouth opened wide, her jaw creaking beneath the strain and the corners of her mouth splitting ever so slightly so that thin rivulets of blood began to run down either side of her chin. From the gaping maw of darkness which was once the mouth of child, a voice began to speak. Its words were old and smelt like dust and sounded like dry leaves scraping over roughened ground.

The air thickened as the words crawled out of Mary's gaping mouth, her white eyes glaring beyond the walls of the inn, faint tears creeping from the edges of her eyes. The passing of time stretched thin, each moment a laborious agony. The voice that spoke through Mary filled the room with a buffeting wind, causing candles to flicker and fight for life, only to be gutted by the gust. The fire in the hearth gasped with one last breath before dying in a cough of white smoke. Through the windows and from beneath the doors, darkness spilled into the common room, filling the space with its inkiness. Only then, did the voice, scraping like the scales of a shedding snake, begin to sound like some form of language. From the top of the stairs, Fee could hear it as clearly as if it were being whispered in his ear. Soon, the hideous crawl of the voice gave way to words of an ancient ilk—words from a language long thought extinct, and if not that, forgotten. Fee could not understand it but he knew it for what it was—the language of the exterminated people. The fae-tongue. He could feel its power coil around him, constricting at the base of his spine and at the top of his neck, commanding he stand at attention whilst such ancient words were spoken. Fee managed to grab onto the banister, or else he would've fallen down the stairs in that rigid stance. If his willpower was strong enough to look away from the girl, Fee was sure he would find the other patrons caught within the same grip of the commanding voice. But it wasn't—the girl held everyone with her whim. A deep enchantment had come over The Candle and Cask, and its ancient source could be felt, from the primeval words that weaved it into being, to the sense of loathing it held for the mortal folk it addressed. Fee could feel the threat behind each word. Dread settled over him, chilling the sweat running down his back.

After what seemed like an eternity, Mary's mouth closed, the mechanics of her jawbone clicking back into place. The thin lines of crimson blood trickling from the corners of her mouth turned her gentle face into a vampiric mask. She glided across the floorboards, the stink of earth and insects following behind her, those alabaster eyes still peering beyond the realms of the living. The doors to the inn creaked open, revealing the pitch black of the night beyond, and into it she went, without so much as a hesitation or a backward glance. As the darkness swallowed Mary, the unerring spell oppressing the inn vanished as quickly as it had come. The smell faded too.

Re-gathering his wits, and summoning what courage still hid in his heart (the thought of his master a strong whip at the back of his mind), Fee raced down the stairs, almost tripping over his own feet. He hurried past the still stunned patrons and Mr. Shaw, in fast pursuit of Mary Shaw. Fear and cowardice barked from the halls of his heart, urging him to turn back, telling him what he had witnessed was enough to summon his master to the village. But there was something else gnashing its teeth within him: the desire; no, the need; no, it was duty that burned inside his chest like a forest ablaze. It was the unrelenting hunting instincts of an inquisitor that pushed him forward, and in that realisation, he found himself closer to his master. Into the night he followed the girl. Up the street, she walked with a swift grace, her bare feet unhindered by the gravel road. In the poor light it seemed like they barely touched the ground. Overhead, a darkening cover of clouds began to creep over the silver disc of the moon and the air tightened with cold. As he moved through the shadows in pursuit, Fee could see the white mist of his breath before his face. From the outskirts of the village faint tendrils of fog began to arise from the ground, spreading and searching. The smell of rot lingered where the girl had been, and with it, there remained an aura of dread. Fee wondered if what he smelt was the scent of fear itself. He moved from house to house, concealing himself in the alleys between the buildings. Ahead, through the gathering fog and failing moonlight, the ominous walls of the woods loomed, the boughs twisted and cruel in the darkness. Mary Shaw moved toward the woods as if the gnarled branches offered her an invitation into that shrouded place. From where he hid, Fee could hear the girl's murmurings. The words of the fae-tongue still came from her mouth, but, unlike the deathly voice that filled the common room, this was Mary's own, and she sang, as if reciting some bygone lullaby. It held a sorrow that struck Fee deeply—a sadness so old it had soured with anger and desperation.

The girl continued up the street, leaving the houses on either side behind. By now, those who were left in the inn came stumbling out onto the street with bewildered looks upon their faces, each looking in a different direction in search of Mary. Fee ignored their confused cries and crept closer to the girl, wading deeper into the terrifying aura which surrounded her. He steeled his heart against it, reciting the teachings of the Citadel over and over again to ward off the fear. The fog continued to gather at an unnatural speed, flooding in from the tree line and smothering the village streets. A particularly thick bank rolled out of the woods right before Mary, the white mass swallowing her entirely. Fee lost sight of her, except for the occasional womanly shadow that shifted with the slightest movement. He could only point to the place the girl now stood by the sound of her voice singing that dreadful song. Bracing himself, he stole into the thick bank, his one hand stretched out before him. He followed the ebb and flow of the girl's voice, but something in it was changing. The pace of the lullaby was slowing down. Mary's voice was beginning to labour, the words drawing out into long breathless syllables. Fee paused to listen. Somewhere ahead of him, the singing faltered, and then... nothing. Silence permeated the fog. Not one sound could be heard. Fee didn't dare move. He could feel his ears straining to pick up any sound, any indication of movement, but it was as if the fog had plugged his ears. Cold sweat broke out across his brow and he could feel his shirt cling to his lower back. Cautiously, he took a step forward. The sole of his shoe crunched against the course road beneath. Ahead, as if in reaction to the sound of his footfall, the fog stirred. At first it swirled in on itself, revealing nothing, but then it parted ever so slightly. There, standing silently in the shroud of white, was Mary Shaw, facing directly at him, those enchanted eyes staring into oblivion. The rivulets of blood had congealed along the sides of her chin. Fee stood his ground and looked into her colourless eyes, hoping to find something within them. The sense of dread was almost unbearable now and the smell of an open grave lingered as heavily as the fog. It took all of Fee's willpower not to turn and run before such terror. He held his ground and looked on at Mary Shaw, but something was off. The silhouette of the girl was oddly misshapen. From behind her left shoulder a strange shadow lurked in the curling fog. It petrified Fee and, although every instinct told him not to shift his stare from the girl's white eyes, he felt his eyes slowly turn toward the strange shape lurking behind Mary Shaw. As his eyes settled upon the unclear apparition, the fog parted like a curtain, revealing the hideous face of a woman— a woman who seemed ancient in years, her visage carved and twisted like a demonic runestone, filled with hatred and the shadow of death. Deep within her bottomless eyes Fee could feel the hag's wish of doom for his soul. From her peeling lips a slime covered tongue slowly protruded like a languorous slug and crept from one side of her bottom lip to the other, leaving a thick trail of spit behind. Fine wisps of grey hair, mere remnants of what once covered the hag's head, trailed over her gnarled skin. Fee noticed her crooked fingers, tipped with black nails, creeping over the girl's bare shoulders. *The hag looked almost childish, skulking behind Mary Shaw in the fog, with that strange grin on her face, revealing teeth as wretched and soiled as her soul. Fee took a step backwards and the hag let off a shrill laugh, but her eyes burned with evil, twisting the childlike smile into an insidious sneer. The shrill laugh continued, rolling out of the ancient woman's mouth like crumbling stone and scuttling spiders. It grew louder until Fee was forced to raise his hands to his ears in a futile attempt to block the woman's foul jubilation. The laughter continued, and from behind those high-pitched cries of malicious ecstasy, the same voice from the common room came crawling out, like rattling leaves through winter branches.*

"Fae'lar Essenta Per'culum," the horrible voice hissed. The breath of it was foul and the smell of decay and disturbed earth was suffocating. It smelt like the dens of the resurrectionists. The three words drove a stake, cold as ice, deep into Fee's heart, and the hag was overcome with another fit of laughter. Her eyes flashed with the pleasure of his fear.

"Fae'lar Essenta Per'culum," the hag hissed again, her crooked fingers strengthening their grip around Mary Shaw's shoulders.

Fee took a step backward and the hag's eyes glared at him one last time. The pleasure from those abyssal orbs was gone. The laughter ceased. The childish expression on her hideous face vanished into the cruel lines that creased her face.

A voice, soft but cruel, whispered in his ear from over his shoulder. "Run."

The word startled Fee and he turned on his heels and ran back down the road, his boots scraping against the gravel and stones. Behind him he could still hear the voice of the witch whisper in his ear, "Run, run, run."

In the deep caverns of his mind he could feel the witch's laugh roll over itself, covering his thoughts with its oiliness. He sprinted down the street, leaving Mary Shaw behind in the fog, fleeing from the hag that hid behind her shoulder. The fog still coiled around his feet when...

"... I regained sight of the inn and the village folk. I had seen the witch of the woods, and her face will never leave me. I left the girl behind too, and fled in fear. I'm not proud of my actions, but there was nothing else I could do. The witch filled me with terror and I could not withstand it."

Blackwood looked at his apprentice's face in the firelight. It was drawn and deep shadows had come to settle in the grooves of his cheeks. In the firelight, he seemed older, much older. Blackwood suspected the witch had taken something from him. *Perhaps a few years of his life, perhaps more, but the witch had helped herself to his lifeblood.* The inquisitor pushed his glass of whiskey across the table and offered it to his apprentice with a gently nod. "You did what you could and saw what you did. And it was enough," Blackwood said with a touch of comfort in his hard voice. "Here we sit, the presence of a witch uncovered."

Fee finished his glass of whiskey and took the one handed to him by his master. "Fae'lar Essenta Per'culum," he recited in a whisper barely audible to either himself, or his master. "Why would she say that to me?"

"It..." Blackwood corrected sternly. "It was taunting you. During the war years and the chaos thereafter, the magic-kind would use the words that persecuted their people as a mantra against the Inquisition. Like a rallying war chant." The inquisitor looked deep into the flames burning in the hearth, his eyes distant with memory.

"A challenge?" Fee asked.

The inquisitor met his stare and nodded. "I believe so."

Blackwood shifted his weight in his chair and folded his legs. "Now, tell me what the girl said in the common room?"

Fee sat forward in his chair, leaning his elbows on the table. He glanced over his master's shoulder again to make sure no one who remained in the common room was eavesdropping. "I can't recall." He paused. "Forgive me, Master Blackwood. I have tried to remember the words, but I cannot. It's strange. If I think of that voice, I can hear the words of that ancient tongue echo in my mind, but as soon as I try to mutter them, or truly recall them beyond their sound in my memory, they disappear like dust in the wind. It is the oddest thing. Perhaps fear still bars entry to those memories. Perhaps in time."

Blackwood rolled his tongue over his teeth as he contemplated the words of his apprentice. "Interesting," he mused.

"What is?"

"I don't think it's fear that prevents you from remembering, although I do not doubt it still resides within your heart. It may be that a spell has been cast upon you. To protect the witch in some way. I'm sure if I'm to ask anyone who was in the inn that night, I would be met with the same answer as yours. Even those of the *Old Ways* were wary of the power their ancient tongue held, and I doubt this witch, if that is what is truly behind what's happening in Westgrave, would risk letting some village folk recite the words it spoke. Not even the oldest *fae* would allow a mortal to speak such words for fear of them muttering something incorrectly. Who knows what horrors a misspoken utterance could summon. No, it is not your fault that you cannot remember what was said."

Fee could feel the inquisitor's eyes search him for any detail that he may have forgotten to tell. Yet, the inquisitor asked no more questions about the girl. Or the witch-thing for that matter. He simply sat for a series of long moments, contemplating everything his apprentice had related to him. In the hearth, a piece of wood let off a loud crack, sending a shower of sparks up into the darkness of the room before collapsing in on itself, spawning another series of flames. Finally, the inquisitor broke his silence. The question was there in his voice, but it was never asked. "You mentioned other developments."

Fee leaned back in his chair—relief filling his face and something of the boyish charm returning to his expression. He was happy to be off the topic of the witch-thing. "Yes, there have been several," he agreed. He took another sip of whiskey before saying more. "Mary, or Ms. Shaw rather, hasn't moved since that night. Not one limb has stirred from the slumber that has taken her. She was found the following morning, lying on the ground where I believe I last saw her standing in the company of that creature. Nevertheless, she has resided in the inn ever since. But what is strange is the weather. The fog has not moved on since that night, neither has the rain. It is as if they and Ms. Shaw are connected."

Blackwood thought about this as his apprentice spoke. *The weather was the domain of the magic-kind. It always had been.*

"Even stranger still, a man came into Westgrave not two days ago. A traveller from Hellendal making his way to Stone Harbour, much like others heading west along the great coastal road. He was a merchant, so he told us, moving from town to town as he made his way in time for his vessel which was set for departure in the coming days. But from my judgement, I put the man closer to a snake-oil salesman than a merchant. I maintained my distance from the man when he arrived in Westgrave, allowing the nervous village folk to consume most of his time. You see, they were desperate to hear of broader events, searching I suppose for some hope that their situation was not entirely hopeless. Or to find some comfort at least that Ms. Shaw's fate was not completely doomed. Upon hearing about Ms. Shaw's condition, this medicine man proclaimed to have come across other cases along his winding route up the coastal road. In fact, he claimed that the last few villages had all been stricken by the same odd occurrence, except that all the girls affected by the ailment were now missing. He named the villages— Heswend, Gorin and Chem—all three no more than a day's ride from Westgrave. In each case, the snake-oil salesman claimed there had been a girl, just coming of age, who had allegedly been struck by an odd sleeping sickness, interrupted by bouts of sleepwalking. He went on to air his sympathies for those towns, stating if only he had been there earlier to sell his tonics, then perhaps the missing girls would still be safe in their homes. You can only imagine the business the man made off the back of that. He barely hesitated to exploit the situation of the Shaws or the people of Westgrave. He nearly sold his entire cache of tonics, and now I can only assume every child in Westgrave is being given a tablespoon of perfumed oils. The hilarity of it."

"*A stranger in the night to herald the Thorn*," Blackwood murmured.

Fee frowned. The ashen look returned to his face.

"*A peddler's dark omens to awaken the Spear*," Blackwood whispered.

"Surely, you can't believe any of this has to do with that old poem," Fee protested, his voice filled with incredulity.

"The texts of the Inquisition do not contain poems of no importance, Fee," he said sternly. The inquisitor's face was expressionless, but his eyes bore the ferocity that set him apart as a wolf amongst men. His voice was harsh, and the rebuke set his young apprentice aback. "You fear the *fae* and their ilk because you know they exist, yet you question the writings that speak of them. Such logic will not see you through the Rites."

The inquisitor's words made Fee nervous. "I do not question the texts. I just struggle to believe that these events can possibly link to a poem of such dark prophecy," the apprentice defended.

Blackwood leaned forward, the shadows of the fires causing mischief along those weathered lines on his face. "How many thousands were lost in the first years of the war because we simply couldn't bring ourselves to accept the impossible? How many innocents did we lose because we would not acknowledge the simple origins of unbelievable power? The *fae* are otherworldly, and their schemes are not brought to fruition by grand plots. They deal in threads, weaving them slowly together until the time is right to strike. No Fee, annihilation is sown from the humblest seed. Do not underestimate what small turn of events can bring about prophecy."

Fee nodded in acquiescence. He completed the poem to acknowledge the inquisitor's point, "*And a messenger to mark the time of the Claw.*"

Blackwood could not help but think of the fallen priest—the Scarolen—at the station in Gotheim. *A messenger to mark the time.* He pushed the thought away and turned back his attention to the matters at hand. "The night is growing old and I would still like to see Ms. Shaw before retiring. About these other three villages, I assume you've spent the last few days productively and investigated the snake-oil salesman's claims?"

"I have. And despite the man's devious sales techniques,

what he said of Heswend, Gorin and Chem is true. A girl has gone missing from each village. Let me just say that the people of those places weren't open to a stranger's prying questions, but I managed to acquire the details of each disappearance. There are slight differences between each girl, but the gist is the same. Each girl was taken by a sleeping sickness—as the salesman would diagnose it—and each one displayed strange bouts of behaviour before disappearing."

Blackwood nodded as he listened to Fee speak. The final pieces of the case of Mary Shaw were beginning to fall into place in his mind. An evident pattern could be accounted for in the area. His apprentice had declared the presence of the *fae* and even claimed to have seen one. He had even heard the ancient tongue of the *Old Ways*. The only thing remaining was for an inquisitor to get to work and uncover the truth of what was happening in Westgrave.

"You've done well, Fee," the inquisitor said plainly. "I couldn't have asked for a more thorough investigation to be done on my behalf." He pushed his chair back, its wooden legs scratching against the floorboards, and stood to face the fire one last time. "But now it's time to pay Ms. Shaw a visit."

5

THE VISITATION

By the time the agents of the Citadel had concluded their counsel *The Candle and Cask*'s common room was deserted. Besides the inquisitor and his apprentice, Mr. Shaw was the only other person left in the inn. The macabre room was now overly populated with deep shadows—the glass-like eyes of taxidermy animal heads staring at the three men from their perches along the walls, a silent audience to the dark business at hand. The fire in the hearth would burn long into the early morning still, and the gold glow from the flames leapt back and forth like the tongues of a mouth to hell.

Blackwood walked to the bar. Fee followed in his master's stride, carrying the inquisitor's letter bag and wide brimmed hat.

The inquisitor placed his hand on the countertop once again and looked at Mr. Shaw with eyes that had seen things blacker than what the darkest imagination could conjure. Beneath the weight of Blackwood's stare, the innkeeper seemed fragile. "I would like to see your daughter, Mr Shaw." His tone of voice was flat and matter-of-fact.

Blackwood could see the conflict of a father behind Mr.

Shaw's eyes. Beads of sweat appeared below the man's hair-line. If only for a moment, the inquisitor allowed the thoughts of a father to weigh the options set before him.

"Mary is sleeping," the innkeeper replied, hoarsely.

On the countertop, the inquisitor's flat hands closed into fists. "And so she has been for days now," Blackwood said. His voice remained steady but even in the poor light of the room, the apprentice at his side noticed the wolfish glint in the inquisitor's eyes.

Mr. Shaw remained still where he stood, facing the hard glare of the inquisitor. A bird against a wolf. Fee could appreciate the man's courage but there was no standing against an inquisitor—and Blackwood was like no other.

Blackwood released a deep breath of air through his slightly opened lips. "Do not let the instincts of fatherhood come between the Citadel and the fate of your daughter. To stand against me is to welcome death. I will see your daughter this evening, Mr. Shaw. Do you deny me?" A sharpness entered his voice as he asked the question.

Mr. Shaw's panic-stricken eyes first glanced at Fee, hoping to find some salvation there, but when he saw nothing but cold temperament in the man's face, he looked back at the inquisitor. The strain in his brow gave way to resignation and his shoulders slumped forward as if a heavy stone had been removed from his neck. "Very well," he muttered. He threw the cleaning cloth—which seemed to be a permanent fixture in his hands—onto the bar counter and made his way toward the staircase. "Follow me, Master Blackwood," he managed, with forced politeness.

The inquisitor and apprentice followed Mr. Shaw up the stairs and onto the landing. Blackwood recognised it from Fee's tale and looked beyond the innkeeper toward the end of the hallway. There, set in the darkness, stood a single door. A glow escaped from its frame, drawing a square of faint light in the dark passage. *The girl's room*. He imagined the girl standing in the dark, bare as the day she was born—as his apprentice had described—her eyes glazed over with an otherworldly sight. In his mind, Blackwood traced her steps down the passageway, past where they stood now and down the stairs. He followed Mr. Shaw down the passageway toward the lone door. The floor was cushioned with a thick carpet and the footfalls of the three men were soft and barely audible, but they stepped as though there was broken glass beneath their feet. Mr. Shaw walked slowly as if trying not to wake his daughter. In the silence beyond his shoulder, Blackwood could hear Fee's breathing grow unsettled. The inquisitor kept his eyes fixed on the door as they approached. On either side, rooms stood closed and no light crept from beneath their doors. They could've been the only people awake in Westgrave. This was not a surprise to Blackwood, taking into account the late hour.

Mr. Shaw paused before the door to Mary's room. Here the air was stale and thick. The innkeeper placed his hand on the doorknob and looked over his shoulder, catching Blackwood's eyes. The father's eyes were wide with fear. "Mary lies inside," he whispered.

Blackwood nodded to him to open the door.

Slowly, Mr. Shaw turned the doorknob and eased the door inward. The sickly light, pale and green in the awkwardly fitting door frame, brightened into a warm glow. The thick air became oppressive, the hint of something foul meeting them at the threshold of the passageway. Mr. Shaw stepped into the bedroom and the other two followed.

It took a moment for Blackwood's eyes to adjust to the brightness of the room. Countless candles stood about the room like distant cities built upon mounds of melted wax.

The army of little flames cast a dancing light about the room. A small fire burned in the fireplace at the far end of the room. Once, this room would have been the inn's fanciest room, reserved for a wealthy merchant or a weary traveller willing to spend a little more coin for some extra comfort. Now, it was the living mausoleum of the Shaw girl. She lay still and asleep upon a bed against the furthest wall. The air was sickly hot. The cumulative heat of the candles and fire made it almost unbearable and, underneath the sweaty air, Blackwood smelled the faint odour of death which seemed to move about in the room. He walked toward the bed, and, as he did, the foulness in the air receded before him. He unbuttoned his coat completely and slipped it off, holding it out for Fee. The apprentice stepped forward and relieved Blackwood of the garment. Blackwood could already feel the sweat gather beneath his arms and in the small of his back. It wouldn't take long until his shirt was soaked through. He was tempted to unbutton his black waist coat, and he would have, if not for the concealed mesh armour sewn into its lining.

Standing over the bed, the inquisitor examined Mary Shaw. A film of perspiration covered the girl's skin and the thin nightgown covering her body clung tightly to her, revealing her developing body. Her hair was combed neatly into a side parting. Blackwood glanced around the room from where he stood. Candles burnt gently on the windowsill. In the corner behind the door stood a chair, still holding the shape of someone's buttocks in the cushion. "Who has been watching the girl?" Blackwood asked in a hushed voice.

Still standing by the door, Mr. Shaw cleared his voice and answered, "My wife, Master Inquisitor. She only leaves the child to gain a few hours of sleep."

Blackwood looked at Fee. The colour had left the young man's face and a dark grey pallid had settled over his thinning cheeks. "Even on the night she left her bed and walked to the woods?" he queried.

Mr. Shaw looked nervously at Fee. "Nay, not on that night. There was nothing odd to say she was anything but sick," the father asserted.

Blackwood turned his attention back to Mary. For just a moment—*he nearly missed it*—the air around the girl was fetid, like a damp grave. Yet, as quickly as he caught it, the smell dissipated. There was something strange in the air. He could feel it pushing on his mind. He examined the mattress surrounding the girl and noticed round stones beneath the blankets. The inquisitor slipped a hand beneath the sheets and placed a hand on one of them. *Warming stones*. He looked at the candles and the fire once again. By now the sweat was trickling down his back, his shirt clung to his waistcoat. Something pulled at the back of his right ear. It was the feeling you get when someone lurked behind you and peered over your shoulder. He tried to push the feeling away, and, as if in response, a breath of foul air blew over his shoulder and into his face. Blackwood turned quickly, only to see Fee and Mr. Shaw watching him intently from the doorway. *Something is wrong with the air here*. He was sure of it. The candles along the shelf above the fireplace fluttered slightly, despite there being no draft. Fee caught the unnatural movement in the air too. The inquisitor was relieved to see his apprentice still in command of his wits. He turned back to the bed and felt another stone. It too was warm.

"To keep her warm," Mr. Shaw called out from the doorway. "No matter what we try, we can't get our Mary warm."

Blackwood did not turn to face the innkeeper. He was examining the girl even closer. Her chest rose and fell with the slight rhythm of deep sleep. Her eyes rolled violently behind her closed lids, moving one way and then the other.

Dreams. Nightmares. Blackwood thought of another possibility. *Visions.* He placed his hand on the girl's bare forearm. From the doorway Blackwood heard Mr. Shaw take a step forward. "Come no closer," he nearly growled, not taking his eyes from the girl. Mary's skin was cold to the touch. He could feel the pulse of blood beneath the softness. There was no sign of death here, but something unnatural was at work. The air behind his ear stirred again and, with it, a sense of dread clawed up his back like little daggers of ice. Blackwood tightened his grip around the girl's arm. Her eyes began to shudder more violently. From behind him, the imposing sense of dread grew stronger, like a whisper reaching for his ear. Blackwood fought against it, squeezing Mary's thin arm, the knuckles of his hand turning white. The dread licked at the nape of his neck, and the foul smell of mould and spoiled flesh hit his cheek. The face of a woman, turned wretched by the long years of age, peering over his shoulder flashed through his mind like a hot razor. He could smell the reek of death come off her black teeth. He could feel it drip from her even blacker tongue as it reached out desperately from her gnarled mouth to lick his ear, her mad eyes rolling upward to the ceiling in languorous pleasure. The image of the woman was so clear, Blackwood could nearly feel the wretch's leathery skin against his neck. He turned on his feet, letting go of Mary's arm, and peered around the room. Mr. Shaw and Fee remained where they had been moments before, except the dread he had felt was worn on their faces like horrible masks. The inquisitor followed their eyes and saw a shadow move across the room, following the line of candle mounds against the far wall. The flames flickered and wavered violently in its wake. The smell of an open grave was ripe now. The scent of upturned earth and rot—ancient and dry—filled the room. The shadow skirted across the wall before vanishing in the darkness behind the bed.

The Old Ways. The image of the haggard woman left his mind as quickly as it had emerged, and the thought of *fae-magic* reinvigorated his fortitude. He turned to face the girl again. The air grew closed, almost suffocating, and the candles scattered about the room began to flicker violently. Blackwood released his grip on Mary's arm and waited. The flames quietened, and the air loosened. The foul odour diminished but it did not leave the room entirely. The inquisitor waited for another moment to be sure of his suspicion. He could touch the girl's arm again to be sure, but his instincts told him that wouldn't be necessary. Years of pursuing magic-kind and the nightmares from its realm had sharpened his hunter's instinct to the point of primitive precognition. There was something in the room, either of, or connected to, the girl that despised his presence in the room and hated his touch on her even more. The inquisitor began to run through the possibilities in his mind. A witch powerful enough to possess a mortal hadn't been heard of, or seen, in decades. That was true magic of the *Old Ways*—powers of the ancient ones, and they were long gone, dead before the end of the war. Yet, an inquisitor never dismissed a suspicion. If a witch of such power was responsible for Mary Shaw's condition, then the Citadel had far darker concerns than what was happening in Westgrave. He thought of the witch Fee had allegedly seen in the fog. *Had he not just felt a haggard presence over his shoulder?* The *Old Ways* worked in strange ways, doing strange things to one's mind. Blackwood focused himself on the situation at hand and pulled his thoughts back from their wanderings. *If not a witch, then what? A shade?* A shade could not hide in such light, despite the dancing shadows cast by the firelight. There was the possibility that the girl was an *inherent.* He gazed over her developing body, following the way the nightgown clung to her perspiring skin, accentuating the curves and bumps of her maturing form. She was of the right age, crossing from being a child into womanhood. *Inherents* were rare too, but Blackwood favoured the odds of this being the cause of the supernatural occurrences in Westgrave, rather than the presence of witchcraft. There was only one way to strip the veil from the true culprit's face. Blackwood pulled the black coin from his trouser pocket and looked at it nestled in the palm of his upturned hand. He watched as faint ribbons of shadow fluttered around its edges as it consumed the light around it. The sigil of the Inquisition —the cross with double arms—was stamped into its surface. The black token was an aged tool of Blackwood's order, one of the first to be created to aid the inquisitors in their hunt for the *fae* and lesser magic-kind. The coin was blessed with holy litanies and was anathema to the otherworldly. He turned it in his hand until it sat between his index finger and thumb. Slowly, whilst maintaining his awareness of the room, Blackwood reached out and held the black coin over the chest of the girl. The air stirred around her and the oppressive presence returned to the room. Beyond the bed, the candles began to flutter in an unseen and unfelt wind. Even the flames in the fireplace seemed to struggle against a phantom wind. The ribbons of shadow thickened around the edges of the coin as the effects of the token began to challenge whatever dark magic was at work in Mary Shaw. The coin grew heavier between his fingers and his arm began to tremble. The wretched smell returned and this time it lingered before Blackwood as if death blew into his face with an open mouth. The stench bloomed from where the girl lay upon the bed. Blackwood strained to keep his hold on the coin and the more it reacted to the unseen magic, the stronger the unknown pres-

ence became, filling the room with its aura of dread. The
candles flickered violently now and the fire in the hearth
shifted between near suffocation and a raging furnace. Light
and darkness struggled against one another. Blackwood
fought to hold the coin before the girl. Whatever ill machina-
tions were at play here, they were strong. Far stronger than
he'd expected. He struggled on. It was only a matter of time
before the black coin overcame the theatrics of devilry. The
stones around the girl began to steam, turning the bedsheets
black with their growing heat. The coin rang between his
fingers and a deep groan, borne from a breathless mouth,
unending in its tormented waking, filled the room. The
phantom wind which harassed the candles and flames
suddenly erupted into reality, carrying with it the smell of
filthy feathers and dried bones. It wailed from each corner,
blowing out every candle and gutting the fire as it reached a
sudden crescendo. Blackwood fought against the urge to put
his hands to his ears. On the back of the wind a foul voice
screamed indiscernible words, but Blackwood took them for
what they were. *Curses*. As the last remnant of light was
vanquished, the wind ceased and there was silence. Candles
rolled across the floor. Smoke drifted in faint blue clouds.
Down the passageway, Blackwood could hear the occupants
in the other rooms begin to stir. He turned quickly and peered
over his shoulder, "Shut the door, Fee," he barked. Whatever
fiend the coin was forcing from its hiding place, the inquisitor
did not want it escaping into the passageway.

At first Fee remained where he stood. The apprentice was
obviously still stunned by the terrible events he just
witnessed. Mr. Shaw was frozen too, paralysed with fear.

"Fee! The door," the inquisitor ordered again, his voice a
deep growl.

This time Fee managed to shake the terror from his limbs.

He reached for the door and slammed it shut. It rocked in its frame and a few flakes of plaster fell to the ground like pale leaves.

A purple twilight filled the room and the heat subsided just a little. Fee turned from the door and rested his back against it. The long sigh of relief which he began to release through pursed lips caught in his tongue as he looked across the room at the bed where Mary Shaw lay. He raised an arm and pointed a shaking finger at something beyond the inquisitor.

Blackwood watched as his apprentice struggled to raise his arm to shoulder height. In the dark, the young man's finger looked like a white wand of bone and flesh. The finger pointed at him, but Fee's eyes looked beyond him, over his shoulder at something behind the inquisitor. Blackwood followed the apprentice's eyes and turned to look back at the bed.

Mary Shaw sat upright in the bed, her pale skin almost luminescent in the strange twilight. Her long dark hair fell in thick cascades down to her lower back. She looked straight ahead with eyes clouded over. A milky storm bellowed within them, shadows shifting in the grey murk. Blackwood leapt to his feet and held the black coin before him like a ward. In the darkness, Mary's head turned on her neck and her waxen face looked up at the inquisitor, those white eyes looking beyond him. Her mouth stretched open, pulling her face at strange angles like soft clay, twisting her soft girlish features into a distorted mask. From the depths of her open mouth a hollow rasp echoed from within her black throat. Abyssal sorcery followed in its wake, conjuring living flame, reigniting the extinguished candles and cold hearth. All at once, the room was alight.

Blackwood took a step forward, wielding the black token

of the Citadel before him. The girl hissed at it, the traces of a scowl wrinkling her twisted face. "Declare yourself," the inquisitor growled. He glared at Mary Shaw, peering deep eyes, challenging whatever lurked behind the enchantment.

Mary Shaw, or the girl that once was her, released a tired laugh from her gaping mouth, scoffing at the inquisitor's order. She placed her hands in her lap and looked about the room, her twisted face creaking under the strain of her stretched-open mouth. The cuts that had begun to heal at the corners of her lips re-opened and fresh lines of blood began to trickle down her chin.

"Stop it, I beg you," Mr. Shaw yelled from his place of paralysis.

Blackwood disregarded his pleas, not knowing if the man's cry was for him or his daughter. He took another step forward. The weight of the coin in his hand was tremendous now as the magic in Mary began to waken. He had experienced such strong reactions between the black coin and the *Old Ways* before, but it never fully prepared him for the strain it put upon him. The power of the coin was only as strong as his mind, as resolute as his will, and he focused his thoughts on it. The force contained within the coin acted like a lodestone to magic and the creatures which possessed it—drawing them from hiding like poison from a wound. Whatever was at work here was reacting strongly to the coin's magnetism. He needed to maintain the connection. If the conduit between the coin and the *Old Ways* were to snap, there would be no telling how things may unravel. At the moment, the token was drawing the magic out of the shadows, but holding it at bay too, like a cage around a wild animal. A sudden break in that bind could send the essence of magic beyond the reach of his power, or worse, unleash it upon the room in a fury. The latter would spell doom for everyone—perhaps even Mary.

Sweat trickled down the inquisitor's temples. He maintained his focus on the coin between his fingers and the distorted face of Mary Shaw. "Reveal yourself," he ordered again, his voice straining beneath the effort to maintain the influence of the coin.

Whatever it was, Blackwood could feel its powerful will press against his, as if his voice was some distant nuisance, Mary Shaw turned her face, her glazed eyes taking in the room and settling on the inquisitor. A voice as dry as winter leaves shambled out of her black mouth. "Declare *yourself*, murderer of children," it sneered. A creaking laugh followed the words like a hollow wind.

Blackwood grimaced. "I am Blackwood, Inquisitor of the Citadel," he declared, "and by the power of this sigil I command you to speak your name."

The black coin pulled at him, nearly sending him off-balance, but he resisted its weight.

"*We* don't declare ourselves to child murderers," the death-like voice exclaimed. A fresh smell of rot came off the back of its retort.

"Speak," the inquisitor barked.

For a moment the girl-like qualities returned to Mary's face and the murky cataracts over her eyes revealed the blue beneath. "I'm Mary Shaw," the girl's voice protested, innocent and sweet compared the rasping one that had preceded it.

From the back of the room her father took a step forward. "Mary," he cried, emotion cracking through the single word.

"Stay where you are," Blackwood commanded, not daring to take his eyes off the girl.

Mary's eyes milked over again, and the gentleness disappeared from her face. The dry laugh cackled from the back of her throat once more. "And you stay where you are, Inquisitor of the Citadel," the voice teased, almost taking on

the sound of Blackwood's voice at it revelled in the word
—*Citadel.*

The candles began to flicker again, and, from behind the
head of the bed, a dark shadow began to grow, consuming the
wall and reaching out like an impenetrable vapour. It gathered
mass and came to a halt just behind Mary's upright back.
Blackwood reached behind his own back and gripped the
smooth wooden handle holstered in his belt.

In an instant, Mary's neck cracked violently as she turned
to address the inquisitor's movement. "Do you not recall the
murder of children," she hissed.

The room wavered for a moment before Blackwood.
Ripples ran along the walls as if a pebble had been dropped
into a pond. The shadow behind Mary turned and shifted and
everything began to fall away. The candles grew dimmer, the
heat from the fireplace dwindled and, beneath him, the floor
vanished as the room began to shrink beneath the growing
mass of the shadow, until there was only darkness …

*It engulfed everything. All around him the abyss stretched.
There were no horizons or ceiling above him. There was no
sign of the room. Fee and Mr. Shaw were gone. Even Mary
had vanished. Blackwood looked down at his feet and saw
nothing but darkness stretched beneath him. He was an island
of existence in an ocean of nothingness. He took a step
forward and felt that his boot found footing on the ground
beneath him, but no sound came from the footfall. He looked
for the black coin in his hand and it was gone. Almost out of
instinct he reached for the wooden handle holstered at the
back of his belt and, again, he found nothing. Whatever this
was, some kind of spell or enchantment, he had been stripped
of his inquisitorial tools. A powerful magic had to be at work*

to not only disarm him, but to displace him into some other-worldly realm. He could feel the weight of dread sink to the bottom of his stomach.

In the stillness of the nothing, Blackwood could feel something approach from the rear. It travelled from a distance, but he could still sense its coming. He thought he could hear it— a faint murmur, like a muffled cry. He turned to face it and heard nothing. He looked into the distance of the never-ending blackness and saw nothing. From over his shoulder he could hear it approach again. Impossible. Approaching from the direction he had just been facing, Blackwood could hear the murmur grow louder as it continued to approach. He turned again, and, as before, it ceased to come from the direction he faced, but instead crept up from behind. The inquisitor listened. Cold sweat gathered in the small of his back. He didn't know the dead to sweat. That was at least a small relief in this strange place. The murmur grew louder, echoing from the distance of the darkness like rolling thunder, gaining speed, getting closer, until it took form and filled the nothing with the rasping laughter of the unknown voice. It came from every direction, mocking him as it cackled through the dark, and then fell silent again.

Blackwood turned, squinting into the darkness that surrounded him. There was something, or someone, here with him. He could feel it. The hunter's instinct was beginning to take control, and he relied more on that now than on his senses. Whatever it was, it moved with extraordinary speed, shifting from one flank to another. He almost thought he could hear the sound of rough material, like clothing, rustle in the darkness. There it was—to his left. And then again to the right. This time followed by a faint snicker of coarse, ancient laughter. Blackwood could hear his heartbeat between his ears. From somewhere up ahead the laugher cracked through the silence like a shrill whip, charging toward him with speed. In his mind's eye Blackwood could see a horribly withered hag charge out of the darkness, her eyes mad with black magic and a wicked tongue dangling out of her mouth. All of this he saw in his mind, but with his eyes there was only the impenetrable darkness. She was close, racing forward in a tattered dress spoilt by blood and filth. Still, there was only darkness before him. At any moment, she would break through the shadows and be upon him—and he would be defenceless against whatever would follow. The dread filled his drying mouth with a sour taste. Any moment now. He braced himself. The darkness before him remained still, unchanged. And then, against his ear, a croaking voice whispered with a foul breath, "Don't you remember?"

Blackwood shuddered at the voice in his ear as cold fear ran down his back, and darkness engulfed everything...

The darkness receded, giving way to a firestorm that coloured the night sky red. A great sea of fire and smoke engulfed a distant town, turning the horizon into an apocalyptic scene of destruction. Whirlwinds of fire, carried by gusts of wind, moved from east to west spreading the inferno to untouched quarters of buildings. Overhead, clouds of smoke and ash converged into massive towers that defied the sanctity of the heavens. Air boiled and the screams of several hundred souls could be heard wailing beneath the raging fires. The cobbled streets cracked and melted beneath the heat of the furnace, the stone bubbling and splitting like wood. By dawn, the town would be reduced to a hellish wasteland of smouldering debris and devastation.

Blackwood watched the scene unfold from a hilltop not far from where the first buildings of the town once stood.

Even from such a distance, he had to raise his hand against the heat.

The voice whispered in his ear once again, "Do you remember?" There was no laughter now, just an overpowering sense of pain and desperation in the words.

Blackwood looked around with eyes that were not his own. He raised hands that were not his own and looked at the gauntlets that covered them. The body he possessed was enclosed in a highly decorated suit of armour. Fine and intricate lines of filigree ran across the breastplate and in the bright orange light cast by the distant inferno, he could make out the images of horrible angels depicted in the metalwork. This was not his body. This was not his memory. Despite these truths, he still felt a distant familiarity to it all, as if he were a fragment of the memory itself, in some way part of the recollection but not entirely present. He recognised the armour adorning the body he possessed—it was the armour of the emperors' honour guard, the Baldirim. How was that even possible? The Baldirim were of another age, legendary warriors of the first War of Religion, the founding fathers of the inquisition.

The inquisitor turned his back to the burning town in the distance. Standing in the strange, fiery twilight was a group of men, other Baldirim, their armour sparkling in the glow of the firestorm spreading across the horizon. None of them looked at him. Blackwood couldn't be sure if he was entirely here ... There ... Or in whatever time and space he found himself. The dark figures ahead stood in a closed cluster, their attention drawn to something at the centre of the hilltop. Whatever it was, it resided beyond the light cast by the distant fires, and beyond his line of sight. Blackwood found himself stepping forward, not out of his own predilection but because this was what the vision, or memory, wanted him to see. This is what he believed. The body that hosted him began to walk across the knoll, its black armoured boots crushing the long grass beneath its heels. Blackwood could feel the cooler night air caress his face. He could still smell ash and smoke and fire upon the breeze but there was a freshness in it too—the faint touch of woodlands and water. The men ahead grew closer as long strides bore him forward. As he approached, the scene before him became clearer. The gathering of Baldirim was a grim audience before the stage of what would be a second burning. The men's faces were hard and cruel, their eyes filled with ruthless hate. Some rested their hands on the pommels of their longswords and others leaned on the shafts of spears—but all their eyes were bent to the same thing. A few feet ahead of them, at the centre of the hilltop, seven stakes stood erected in the ground. Bound to each stake was a girl no older than her adolescent years—no older than Mary Shaw.

"Do you remember now?"

The voice whispered in his ear again, this time the words contained a sense of urgency rather than hostility. It urged him on, both in mind as well as body—or at least the host body he now possessed. The armoured golem moved closer, joining the cluster of honour guards before the seven stakes. From here Blackwood could see each girl plainly. They were strikingly beautiful in their own way—one had hair as violent as fire, another's was the colour of ash, even though age had not yet touched her face. Once, before their faces had been beaten, the seven girls had been beautiful; but now the girls were broken and bloody, tied to their own unlit pyre. At the base of each stake were bundles of kindling. The Bildirim at the head of the group turned and faced those behind him. For a moment his eyes paused on Blackwood and met his stare. The man's eyes were unfeeling in a face scarred by war. He gave each of his companions a slight nod before approaching the girls. The others returned the gesture and followed. It was only then that Blackwood noticed each man also carried a jar. Even he carried a jar. His host-body stepped forward and made for one of the girls to the left of the hilltop.

The voice questioned him again. "Do you remember?"

Blackwood answered in his mind, "This is not my memory. I do not know this."

His host-body stopped before the stake and Blackwood looked through a stranger's eyes at the girl bound before him. Her legs were cut and bruised, the dress she wore torn and marred with blood and filth. Mottled dirt and twigs mangled her hair and blood still flowed from the wounds on her face. Welts and bruises still swelled across her cheeks and brow. Yet, despite her condition, the girl's eyes were clear and aware. There was no fear in her eyes. Just an untamable wilderness that looked down at Blackwood with contempt. The host-body lifted the jar and began to pour its contents over the kindling and when it seemed empty, the golem cast the last dregs over the girl's feet. Oil.

Again the voice whispered in his ear, this time almost pleading for him to remember.

"I do not know this memory," the inquisitor answered. Although he spoke true of this memory, that was not his own, let alone of his own age. This was a bygone memory, a recollection from another life that was now being imposed upon his mind. And yet, despite its archaic origin, Blackwood knew what he was witnessing. Baldirim. A town struck by ruin and girls beaten and tied to the stake. This was a purge. Probably just one of a thousand carried out during the Wars of Religion. For the emperor's sake, how many purges had he been a part of?

The host-body withdrew from the stake and rejoined the

other Baldirim. The one who seemed to be the leader of the group gathered a torch from one of the others and began to walk from stake to stake, pausing only long enough to dip the head of the torch into the kindling and let the oil catch alight.

One.

Two.

Three.

Blackwood counted as each pyre caught alight, the flames starting slowly in the dry kindling, gathering their appetite, until the oil burst into fire. By the time the seventh pyre was lit, the first few were fully ablaze, the girls bound to them completely engulfed in hungry flames. Screams wailed over the roar of the fires and sickly black smoke began to pollute the fresh hilltop air with the smell of charred flesh and burnt hair. The girls' screams grew louder. Some fought against the fireproof binds that kept them tied to the stakes, whilst the others simply accepted their fates and succumbed to the immolation. The inquisitor watched the burning and understood. This was a victory—one against the Old Ways and the evils it had brought onto the people. These magic-kind would no longer plague villages and the land men tended to with their foul curses. Yes, this was a victory.

The voice came from inside his head this time, wailing louder than all the girls given to the fire. "DON'T YOU REMEMBER, KILLER OF CHILDREN."

Blackwood reached for his, or rather the host-body's, head, but the arms and hands did nothing. The voice echoed in his mind, shrieking in pain and grief, and beneath that, a harsh anger began to arise. An ancient anger. Blackwood could feel it. Beyond the stakes, on the edge of the glow from the burning pyres, Blackwood caught the glimpse of a woman. She was hard to see through the darkness and the dancing flames and thickening smoke, but he could make out her shape on the far end of the hilltop. She stood still, and although her face was hidden in shadow, Blackwood could feel her eyes upon him, her glare boring into him, looking beyond the shell of the host-body and into the depths of his soul. The anger and hatred in her stare tainted his soul. "Killer of children," she hissed, the dry scraping of her ancient voice cutting through his mind. "Killer of children," she repeated.

There was nothing Blackwood could do to keep her voice out of his mind. Whatever memory or enchantment this was, he had no power within it.

"Killer of children." Her words echoed in his mind.

"Killer of..."

Fee stood helpless as he watched the shadow grow from the head of the bed, stretching along the walls as it gathered mass. It paused just behind Mary, heaving and twisting on itself. The girl had turned all attention onto Blackwood and, from where Fee stood, the inquisitor seemed to be battling against the will of some unseen force. His one hand remained stretched out before him, the black coin of the Citadel gripped between his fingers. Fee could see the inquisitor's grip struggle to hold on the coin, as if it weighed more than he could bear. Blackwood's other hand reached behind him and held the polished wooden handle of the *sharur* holstered on the back of his belt. Whatever was happening in the room, the inquisitor felt it necessary to reach for that horrible weapon. The thought sent a new wave of fear through Fee. Behind him, Mr. Shaw had gone silent, petrified with terror. All about the room the candles flickered violently and the fire in the hearth raged with an unnatural rhythm, the flames stuttering in and out of existence. He hadn't gone through the rites to become an inquisitor yet, but he could feel the presence of the *Old Ways* gather in the room. He could feel its oiliness on his skin. He could hear its voice within his mind, turning his thoughts against him. It would be only a matter of time before its touch sent his mind down a maddening gyre. This is what they had been taught at the Citadel, and now he was feeling the effects of the ancient magic firsthand. He gathered his thoughts and reinforced his willpower, concentrating on his identity. The best defense against the *Old Ways* was to hold onto yourself. It wouldn't stop the poisoning of the mind, but it would hold its crippling effect at bay for a little longer. Fee held onto this. He focused on his willpower and began to push the magic out of his mind.

Across the room, Fee could see Mary's white eyes burrow into the inquisitor and, from her stretched mouth, the words of the ancient *fae-tongue* came shambling out in a languorous drawl. He had no understanding of it, but he could feel its strength and power, and knew it to be a spell. Blackwood appeared frozen where he stood, his one hand still resting on the handle of the *sharur*, and the other still grasping onto the coin between his fingers. The inquisitor had not moved in some long minutes, Fee realised. There was no knowing what enchantment the girl had cast upon him, but if Mary was to lunge for his master, or worse, if the writhing shadow stretching from the bed decided to pounce, Blackwood would be defenceless. Fee took a step forward, breaking the shackles of fear around his ankles. He took another step. If he could reach the inquisitor and grab the *sharur* perhaps they'd stand a chance. The *sharur* was bound to Blackwood, and he had no idea what would happen if he were to take hold of it, but he hoped the hallowed weapon would recognise his need to use it. If it allowed him to handle it, and not strike him or punish him with death, he would cut the girl down. At that moment, as the thought of murdering Mary Shaw crossed his mind, the shifting darkness behind the girl slowed in its movements. Mary maintained her unyielding stare upon the inquisitor, but from the shadow behind her, filthy fingers—wrinkled and stained black—emerged. Ten gnarled fingers crept out of the darkness, five coming to rest on Mary's youthful shoulders. Ragged nails cut through the fine nightgown and dug into the girl's skin, drawing delicate droplets of blood through the thin material. Fee paused at the sight and a hot flash of panic ran through him. The strength of the *Old Ways* whipped at his mind, and for a moment, his courage faltered. He took another step forward, concentrating what will remained in his heart on the *sharur* hanging from his master's belt. The shadow stirred and then paused again. From behind Mary's head, emerging from the shadow, was a horrible face—the same haggard face he had seen in the fog. As it emerged it looked at him with malicious eyes—dark orbs that shone with a gleeful hatred. The lower half of the wrinkled face was twisted with a sickening smile of black teeth. The hag licked at her leathery lips with a fat dark tongue as she stared at him with sordid glee. Fee couldn't be sure if it was with hunger or pleasure that those horrible eyes looked at him, but he knew his death lay at the end of either desire. He stopped mid-step and the hag's smile widened further, revealing gums coloured by decay. Her wicked fingers tightened around Mary's shoulders and the thick tongue slipped back into the wretched mouth. She stared at Fee and laughed with evil delight. "Fae'lar Essenta Per'culum," she whispered and then laughed again, this time the black tongue falling out of her mouth and rolling over her lips.

Fear gripped Fee and he could do nothing before the hag. She stared at him with insidious delight and he could feel

himself become aroused, despite feeling nothing but repul-
sion. She laughed again and taunted him with the inquisitor's
declaration. Her laughter echoed through the room and
grasped at the walls of willpower he had managed to build
around his mind. The sense of arousal continued to grow
despite the sickening feeling that lined his stomach, and,
beyond that, there was something worse. Fee could feel it
emanate from the hag like a lance of pure hatred—and then
he knew it was not hunger or pleasure that filled her dark
eyes but a raw and desperate desire to kill him. She laughed
at him again as if she could sense the realisation dawning
across his mind. Death —this was what that face wished for
him. She slowly began to recede back into the shadow, the
grey wisps of hair disappearing into the darkness first, and
then those terrible eyes vanished, until the ridge of the ancient
nose was the last part to be swallowed by the shadow.

The scene upon the hilltop faded into that place of abyssal
darkness and, after a long moment in time, the room in *The
Candle and Cask* came into view again. At first the walls
were distant, barely visible and there was no floor beneath
Blackwood's feet, but with each breath the walls got closer
and the room more tangible. The light from the candles began
to chase the darkness away and the nothingness which ruled
that place gave way to Mary Shaw's bedroom.

Mary Shaw appeared before Blackwood like a spectre
from a dream. She emerged out of the darkness, her white
eyes still gazing at him. His eyes caught the slightest movement below Mary's face and saw the tips of hideous fingers
disappear into the swirling shadow behind the girl. The
shadow pulled away, shrinking back into the corner of the
room, before finally disappearing behind the bed. The unnat-

ural stuttering of the fire in the hearth steadied and the imposing presence which had pervaded the room disappeared. Mary Shaw fell back onto the bed, her eyes rolling shut as her head hit the pillow. Fine trickles of blood marred her chin and, from what he could see, there appeared to be ten blood spots lined across her shoulders—the nightgown slightly torn in each of those places.

Blackwood lowered the black token, the weight of it no more than a regular coin, and removed his hand from the *sharur*. He glanced over his shoulder and found Fee halfway across the room, paused mid-stride with a deathly expression upon his face. "Fee," he called. His voice was dry and strained.

Fee did not react immediately to his master's call. Blackwood called his name again, and only then did he snap out of the trance which held him. The young man's face was drawn and pale.

The inquisitor walked across the room and took Fee by the shoulders. "What happened here?"

Fee shook himself and met his master's stare. "Did you not see her?"

Blackwood looked back at the girl lying on the bed and knew it was not Mary Shaw that his apprentice was referring to. "The witch. She was here," Blackwood whispered to himself, the sight of the crooked fingers disappearing into shadow now replaying behind his eyes.

"She was barely three feet from you," Fee exclaimed.

"I believe you, Fee. I saw her too," Blackwood assured. He looked back at the girl again, still trying to make sense of what had happened to him, still trying to understand what he had seen. "I just didn't see her in this room," he finally said, turning to meet his apprentice with a hard stare.

Bewilderment lightened Fee's face. There were rare occasions that he dared to question his master's sense, and this was one of them. "What do you mean?"

Blackwood dismissed the doubt he saw in his apprentice's eyes. It was understandable—his mind was still coming to terms with it all. Despite the decades of hunting magic-kind, this was not something he had encountered before. Images from the memory, at least that's what he thought he had witnessed, flashed across the back of his eyes. "Some things are better left unsaid until dawn."

6

AN INQUISITOR RESTS

Blackwood sat by the window and looked out at the bank of fog that clung to the side of the inn. It was good to be in the company of his own thoughts, especially after all that had transpired in the room of Mary Shaw. The presence of the *Old Ways* dissipated quickly once the girl fell back onto the bed. The foul stink of an open grave vanished and the natural state of things seemed to be restored. The inquisitor and apprentice had discovered Mr. Shaw unconscious on the floor by the bedroom door. The man was terrified, as any mortal who had faced such strange happenings would be, and it took some time before Fee could settle the man and bring him to his senses. Blackwood asked the man a few questions once he seemed to calm down, but Mr. Shaw couldn't remember anything beyond the emergence of the shadow from behind the bed. Blackwood believed him, and the inquisitor suspected the loss of memory to have something to do with the witch. At first, he had doubted whether or not a witch was at work in Westgrave, despite his apprentice's reports. Witches were rare in this age and there were countless other manifestations of the *Old Ways* that could explain what was happening to Mary Shaw. The recent events had changed everything. Blackwood was sure of the witch's presence now, and he rebuked himself for ever being doubtful. *Perhaps he was getting too old for this dark work.* From what little detail Fee had told him whilst they were still in the girl's room, and comparing that to his own encounter, the witch's visitation appeared to be different for each of them. Simply considering the nature of his visitation, Blackwood feared the extent of the witch's power.

Once Mr. Shaw appeared cognisant enough, the inquisitor forced the man from the room and asked to be shown his lodging. It took some patience and coercion to get the man to cooperate, but in the end, no one could refuse or hinder the wishes of an inquisitor. There was little else that could be done at such a late hour, and Blackwood needed time to examine everything that had happened. More specifically, he wanted to go over the strange vision. Despite the devilry behind the enchantment, Blackwood believed there was some truth in it— perhaps a clue to the true identity of the witch or even something the fiend wanted him to see. And then there were the witch's words. *Killer of children. Child-killer.* The words repeated in his mind. How many children had been killed by his hand? It was a long time since he had stopped counting the number of magic-born children he'd pulled out of hiding and put to judgement. There were the *inherents* too, all children in their own right. More child than adult in most cases. There had been so many over the years, he'd forgotten their faces. *Yes, he was a child-killer. But all done in the name of the emperor is holy work.* Those last words sounded hollow as he justified his work for the Citadel. They seemed to lose more substance as the years passed. The murder of children, regardless of the cause, was dark work. Yet, what he saw in that vision, was not his memory. Was it the memory of the Baldirim he seemed to possess? Surely that wasn't possible. He absentmindedly looked out at the gloom as he pondered these questions. Regardless of the answers, he knew the magic used to conjure that vision was old and powerful, and, if he listened to the growing alarm in his heart, he feared one inquisitor and an apprentice would not be enough to solve the problem in Westgrave.

Blackwood stood up from the chair and walked away from the window. The room was simple but good enough for what he needed it for. Fatigue was beginning to creep into his limbs and he could feel the itch of sleep grow behind his eyes. The inquisitor's letter bag stood against the bedside table, neatly placed out of the way, and his coat and hat hung on the back of the door. The only thing out of place in the small, but comfortable room, was the glyph drawn with white chalk across the floorboards of the bedroom. Blackwood had traced it shortly after closing the door of the bedroom for the evening. The last thing he had seen before the door closed upon its hinges was the terrified eyes of Mr. Shaw glaring at him from the darkness of the hallway. There was anger and hate in them too. The glyph across the floor would act as a ward against intruders. Anyone, or anything, that entered the room without his permission would trigger the ward and a siren loud enough to crack the windows would be set off. He couldn't be sure of the actions of Mr. Shaw. Not that he would get much sleep this night. But the last thing Blackwood wanted was to deal with a father, driven to madness by fear and love, sneaking into his room and trying something foolish. And Mr. Shaw was not the only person in the inn to concern him. Mary was a threat too. He'd locked the door to her room before leaving, and the key now lay on his bedside table, but still, there was no certainty what the girl was capable of. Especially under the influence of a witch. The ward would stop any attempt by the *Old Ways* to enter the room.

The inquisitor walked over to the table standing against the wall and placed the black coin from his trouser pocket upon its surface. The token was light and normal in all regards, the absence of magic reducing it to nothing but a dark coin. He held his fingers over it for a moment, just to be sure there were no vibrations in it. Stiffness had already settled in the forearm of the hand that held the coin against Mary Shaw earlier. The black coins of the Citadel had been the first tools crafted for the Inquisition's war against the *fae*. He sat at the table and put the *sharur* down alongside the black coin. The *sharur*, crafted from the wood of the great tree Melendle, was the dreaded weapon of an inquisitor, equally feared by people and magic-kind. If anything were to enter his room, Blackwood would be sure have the *sharur* ready. The inquisitor walked over to his letter bag, and from a concealed sleeve, withdrew a thick tome bound in black leather. It was a hallowed book and, pressed into the cover, was the venerable symbol of the Citadel—the double cross enclosed by a ring. It was a rare copy of the dark grimoire known as *Malleus Maleficarum*, the handbook of the Inquisition. Blackwood returned to the table with the heavy book cradled in his hands and took a seat. He put the book before him and, as he stared at the embossed symbol on its cover, Blackwood recalled the sequence of the vision once again, interrogating each element. There was the place of nothingness where only darkness resided. Cold dread quickly followed after thoughts of that place. He was certain it was part of the spell cast upon him, but there was a part of him that believed it to be a real place. It was a ludicrous thought, but it stayed with him nonetheless. Then came the visions of the town consumed by fire and ash, the Baldirim and the purge upon the hilltop. Blackwood slowed the scene as it unfolded behind his eyes one more time. Seven girls, all tied to stakes and put to death. The Baldirim, the honour guard of the emperors, had ceased to exist even before the end of the second War of Religions. They had all been annihilated in the defence of the last emperor—Pangallion —at what was now known as the *Tylean Massacre*. The presence of the Baldirim in the vision, if any of it could be considered true at all, put the scene at least a century ago.

With practiced care, Blackwood opened the codex and turned its pages. He trawled through its chapters, scanning over diagrams and articles drafted in black ink. The grimoire possessed the dark history of the *Old Ways* and all the secrets of its legions. Blackwood paged over chilling sketches of demonic fiends and perilous imps. He looked over the notes on warlocks and druids and all manners of perversion conjured by their foul powers. It was the accounts of witch-craft he was after. Tediously, he compared the vision to the secret history of witches and sorcerers in the *Malleus Malefi-carum*, looking for an anchor that could explain what the witch had shown him. The last hours of the night slowly passed when he came upon an account that touched on the vision. *The Seven Sisters*. He read the trailing handwriting slowly as it chronicled the destruction of an entire town by firestorm and the execution of seven witches. It was a tale that every inquisitor knew—one told and learnt from the time when the ancient *fae*, strongest in the *Old Ways*, still walked the earth. A cold shiver ran through Blackwood. How did he not recognise the details in the vision before? If this witch had anything to do the Seven Sisters, then he was certain he and Fee could do little to save Mary Shaw. Yet, he would try. It was his duty as an inquisitor. Even if it meant facing his own doom. He closed the grimoire and gripped the handle of the *sharur* before standing from the table. He glanced out the window one last time, the incessant irritation of fatigue clawing at the back of his eyes. The witch's voice still haunted him. *Killer of children.* Those words taunted him. Blackwood withdrew to the bed and lay down on top of the blankets. The mattress was soft and he welcomed what small pleasure the comfort gave his weary body. He peered through the darkness at the ceiling above and traced the fine cracks that across the plaster. Sleep came quickly, although it was shallow and restless, and the last thought that crossed his mind as he succumbed to its embrace was the vengeance of a mother.

7

CONVERSATIONS IN THE FOG

The next morning in Westgrave was sullen. The suffocating blanket of fog still hung over the town and, beyond the windows of the inn, the white gloom seemed implacable. By the time the inquisitor and his apprentice sat to take their breakfast—bread, sausages, eggs and coffee—the common room was trembling with whispers. Those who sat at the scattered tables stared at the two men unashamedly. By the looks on their faces, not only had the news of an inquisitor spread —as Blackwood suspected—but it appeared that the events in Mary Shaw's room had also reached the ears of everyone. Mr. Shaw hunkered behind the bar as he had the night before, the red lines of a sleepless night ringing his eyes. His face was grim and resigned, and although he served the men, he did so with disdain, as if they were the cause of his daughter's cursed condition. Blackwood was used to it. This was the treatment fitting for an inquisitor. After all, they were heralds of dark omens and traders in death. He ignored the man's disposition, as well as the stares of the other village folk. The fate of Mary Shaw was still uncertain. He had come to believe the girl was a mere pawn in the schemes of the witch, but he still could not rule out the possibility that the girl herself had come to inherit the powers of the *Old Ways*. Either way, a shadow hung over the girl, and he knew it would be by his hand that her fate would be determined. From the looks of it, everyone else had come to realise this too.

The two men kept to themselves and ate their breakfast in silence. Fee looked worn, the youth gone from his face, and his usually-combed hair was now unkempt and hung over his brow in thick brown curls. The young man hadn't bothered shaving either, a healthy grain of stubble covering his jawline. Blackwood had little sleep. What rest came to him was disrupted by nightmares. He kept dreaming of the girl tied to the stake—her face beaten, her clothes torn—and the fire that consumed her from the toes up. It was the same nightmare, repeating itself, always ending with the face of the witch, hidden at the edge of the firelight. *Killer of children*. He felt as tired as Fee looked, but he suppressed the fatigue. There was a lot more to be demanded of he and his apprentice before they could leave Westgrave. This he knew. It was only a question of how quickly the sequence of the coming events would unravel. Apart from nightmares, other things had come to him while he tossed and turned. During the night he had stitched together everything he had come to learn from Fee and the visitation in Mary Shaw's room. He held little doubt that his assumptions would more likely be true than false.

Blackwood sipped his coffee and scraped the last piece of bread through the remnants of the egg on his plate and put it in his mouth. Whether innocent or *inherent*, Mary Shaw was at the heart of the witch's scheme, and although that remained hidden for now, he was sure the witch would stop at nothing until the girl was completely in her possession. Taking into account the stories of the travelling peddler, the witch had already taken three other girls into her possession. Darker than all these things, Blackwood hoped his deepest suspicions weren't true. The tale of the Seven Sisters picked at him. There were many things he needed to speak to Fee about, and none of it he wished to discuss within the common room of *The Candle and Cask*.

The inquisitor poured the dregs of his coffee into his mouth and swallowed with a grimace. The dark brew was mostly burnt, nowhere near the quality he was used to in Gotheim, but he'd need the drink's medicinal qualities to hold the fatigue from the last night at bay. Fee had barely touched his food, pushing pieces of sausage and bread around the plate like a spoilt child. The boy still had a long way to go before he was ready to take his rites, and if they were to see through to the end of the strange happenings in Westgrave, perhaps his apprentice would be one step closer. He hoped, at the very least, Fee's fortitude would be more resolute. He pushed his chair away from the table and stood up, taking his wide brimmed hat from the back of the chair. "Follow me, Fee. The morning air would do us good," he said flatly. The hardness in his voice carried through the common room, silencing the hushed whispers amongst the village folk. The morning air would do them good, but he was growing tired of the stares from the locals and there was much for them to discuss.

Outside the inn, the air was cold and damp from the fog. Visibility was poor and what little sunlight managed to pene-trate the weather cast an ethereal twilight. Only a few feet could be made out ahead of them, and Blackwood looked out at the cobbled road disappearing into the white beyond. To his left he could see the line of lamps, now unlit, disappearing into the distance too. Little of the village could be seen in the grey, and it felt like they were the only two living souls in the place. No sounds carried through the unnatural weather. *The weather was always in the realm of witches.* The inquisitor spat into the fog and placed his hat on his head. In the poor light, the wide brim cast a deep shadow over his face. He walked down the stairs leading to the street and his apprentice followed. The two men walked in silence up the road, their boots scraping against the cobbled ground. To either side, houses passed by like moored ships on distant banks, the windows shuttered against the weather.

When it seemed safe to talk without the risk of eavesdroppers, Blackwood looked at his apprentice from beneath the brim of his hat. "Tell me Fee, what did you see last night?"

As the two men made their way up the main road of Westgrave, wading through the fog, Fee recounted his experiences of the past night to his master. He spoke of the spell Mary had cast on the inquisitor, he told of the shadow and how the witch emerged from the darkness. He left little detail from his account of the events, and the more he spoke, the better he felt, as if every word expelled the fear in his heart. The inquisitor could also sense the young man's composure return as he told his story, and Blackwood kept his tongue, even though some parts of the apprentice's tale sparked questions. He found it particularly interesting how the witch had appeared to him in the same manner twice, hiding behind Mary Shaw, announcing her intentions more aggressively each time. Fee blushed as he mentioned his arousal, but Blackwood comforted him, discarding it as nothing more than an effect of her magic.

Fee concluded his account and Blackwood picked up the baton and began to tell his apprentice of his experience. Like Fee, he left out no detail, explaining to the young man how the spell had overcome him. He spoke of the place of nothingness and of the vision upon the hilltop. The air seemed to grow cooler and the fog thicker as the inquisitor spoke of these things. Fee wrapped his coat closely around his chest and listened intently to the words of his master. It was only when Blackwood's words fell silent and stopped along the road that Fee realised where they were. Fee looked around, and although he could barely see through the walls of white around them, he recognised where they stood. The inquisitor had led them to the place where Fee had first seen the witch on that night not so long ago. Fee looked at Blackwood with apprehension. The inquisitor had been leading them here the whole time.

Against the white murk surrounding them, the inquisitor looked like a dreadful revenant, his dark eyes gleaming from beneath the brim of his hat, and after long moments of silence, as if contemplating his words, Blackwood spoke. "What do you know of the Seven Sisters?" His voice was hard and alien in the otherworldly surroundings. The inquisitor looked into the fog, his eyes casting a distant stare as if he could see what lurked beyond its curtain.

Fee remained quiet. The name of it sounded familiar, like the name of a person that eluded the tip of the tongue. *The Seven Sisters*. He repeated it over and over again, rolling it from one corner of his memory to another, and then it dawned upon him. "Yes, I recall that story. It's one told to all children, to set the fear of witches into their bones."

Blackwood took a step forward and, with a gentle turn of his hand, he motioned Fee to follow. He looked ahead into the fog, hands folded behind his back, and a solemn tone came over his voice as he began to speak. "The tale of the Seven Sisters is both known and unknown. Known simply because of the commonalities it shares with every other tale from the dark ages. Witches put to the stake and set alight in the name of the emperor. It's a tale as common as a child's fear of bugbears. After all, the purge of witches is a household story, is it not?"

Fee nodded, both his hands tucked into the pockets of his coat. "As common as the tale of an inquisitor skulking into the crypts to vanquish the sleeping undead," the apprentice agreed.

Blackwood made a strange sound, and for a moment, Fee took it to be the beginning of a laugh. The inquisitor never laughed though. He cleared his throat again. "The undead never sleep. The darkness of the underground is a mere sanctuary," he said matter-of-factly.

This time Fee managed a short laugh. His master was incapable of humour. Perhaps he would become the same once he survived the Rites. It was said the Rites had strange effects on those who came out the other side.

Blackwood's raised eyebrow reigned in the apprentice's wandering thoughts. This was no time for laughter, and perhaps that was his apprentice's strongest attribute. The inquisitor continued at the pace he set, following the cobbled road as it began to bend up a gentle slope. "Tales, like those shared amongst villagers and townsfolk, tales about witches and undead hold little truth. They are merely rumour and conjecture. The tale of the Seven Sisters is different. No matter which version you hear told, and there are many for a tale as old as this, the same truths lie at its heart."

"Truths other than what are told in the tale?" Fee asked.

Blackwood shot the apprentice a look that would have caused any other man's stride to falter. "And what are those," Blackwood questioned. The young man had a sharp mind and, although he may still hesitate before the horrors of the *Old Ways*, he never paused before asking a question.

"The Seven Sisters," Fee recited, as if he were a child again, "or rather the story of how seven witches were pulled from the wilds surrounding Megen and put to the stake for their use of black magic and practice in the *Old Ways*."

"In the broadest strokes, that is correct," Blackwood countered. "That is the tale known by villagers and towns-folk. The tale told to frighten children. But there are truths to the tale that are only known by the Citadel, written in the pages of the *Malleus Maleficarum*."

Fee dared to give his master a doubtful stare. The inquisi-tor's referral to the black codex of the Inquisition, the darkest grimoire in possession of the order, was enough to raise alarm bells in his mind. After months in the service of Blackwood, he had come to learn his master's ways, and, if he had learnt anything, the inquisitor was working his way towards linking whatever he had to say about the Seven Sisters with what they were dealing with here in Westgrave. If that was the case, and if what they were to face was the subject of any texts held within that black codex, Fee could do nothing to stop the shiver that crawled down his back.

"Seven witches, burned at the stake," the inquisitor continued, "that is true. But pulled from the wilds, no that is not. The witches, and all sisters to each other in blood as well as magic, were found in the town of Megen. Not in the wilds surrounding it. By the time the hunting force caught the trail of the sorceresses and followed the plague left in their wake, those men who could still bear arms found the women in control of the town, ruling as queens over the folk they had enslaved there. It is written that the townsfolk, under the domain of the witches' foul enchantments, took to eating each other, stringing what remained of the dead along the streets as monuments to their new rulers. The Baldirim who led the hunting party, finally made their way to the witches by fighting their way through the thralls that were once the free people of Megen and capturing the witches. The horrors witnessed in the town were so abominable, the Baldirim captain ordered the town to be burnt to the ground. Not one brick would be left untouched by the flames. By the time the sun rose on the desolation of Megen, all seven witches had joined the clouds of ash that soured the morning sky."

The road began to flatten out again as the two men continued to walk. By now, the houses were becoming fewer, the intervals between their dark hulks in the fog becoming more pronounced.

"Your vision," Fee exclaimed. "What you saw last night was a vision of what happened in Megen."

"I believe so," Blackwood agreed in a hushed tone.

"But it doesn't make sense," the apprentice argued. "What would the events in Megen, or anything that happened so long ago, have anything to do with Mary Shaw and Westgrave?"

The young man's questions were valid and, despite what theories he could come up with to link Megen to the witch at hand, Blackwood could not give his apprentice an answer. "I do not know," he finally admitted. "But whatever it is, the she-devil we encountered last night found it apt enough to break her shroud to show me what she did. Perhaps it's a warning. Or perhaps she did not mean to reveal so much to me at all—that could have been the work of the coin."

Fee's mind worked furiously, trying to make sense of the tale of Megen—as his master had told it—and everything else they had encountered. "The peddler at the inn spoke of three other girls who had been taken by the witch. Mary Shaw, should we fail, would be the fourth …"

Blackwood looked at his apprentice and watched as the young man worked through his thoughts. A different approach to the same set of facts may prove to be fruitful. *A fresh set of eyes*, as they would say.

When the inquisitor did not interrupt him, Fee continued along his line of thought. "What if this witch is looking to collect sisters, perhaps not in the purest sense of bloodline, but in the ways of magic; in the workings of the *Old Ways*?"

Blackwood nodded, encouraging his apprentice to continue.

"What if she's gathering? You've always taught me that those true in the *Old Ways* are sensitive to those who are to become *inherent*. As if they're attracted to those souls in some way, like bees are drawn to nectar. As much as we know the old tales, so do the magic-kind, surely? What if she's looking to recreate the tale of the Seven Sisters?"

Blackwood paused and turned to face Fee, the inquisitor's breath appearing before his face in a faint cloud that barely stood out against the fog. "And what if she's simply preying on the innocent to feed her own power?"

Fee had heard of bats that did something similar, drinking the blood of livestock for food. It was easier to think of a witch acting alone that it was to think of the birth of an entire coven—but then, the *Old Ways* worked in ways stranger than men could understand. "So, what do we do now," he asked of Blackwood.

The inquisitor paused and pointed ahead. "Now, we wait," he said flatly.

Ahead of them, the fog seemed to swirl with the movement of air, as if a breeze disturbed its all-encompassing cover. Through the drifting white, Fee could make out tall structures, too irregularly shaped to be man-made, looming before them. *Trees.* As the silent wind moved the curtain of fog along its current, breaks appeared, and Fee could see the dark trees, twisted and gnarled, stand before them like an ancient wall. The hooked and ragged branches reminded him of the witch's terrible fingers and another shiver ran down his back. Blackwood peered into the gloom with intent—his dark, brooding eyes looking for something within the deep shadows of the tangled boughs.

Fee shifted nervously. "Wait for what?"

Blackwood revealed the black coin of the Citadel resting in the palm of his hand and considered it for a moment. "The witch knows I am here, and she knows that I bring with me the power of the Citadel. She will not wait long to take its prize."

"Mary Shaw," Fee confirmed.

Closing his fist around the coin, the inquisitor nodded and then placed it back into his pocket. "It may not be this evening, or the next, but it will come soon enough. It knows that the longer I have to whittle away at the spell that holds the girl, the less power it will have to control the girl's soul. And if it waits long enough, its power to fight against my authority will be too far diminished to be of any consequence."

The air suddenly felt colder and the shadows amongst the veiled boughs seemed all the more menacing. Of what could be seen beyond the drifting banks of fog, the woods looked like a dreadful place. Thick trunks grew upward, their heavy branches entangling with one another like roots, so that one tree seemed to grow into another. Great mounds of roots rose and fell from the ground like the backs of burrowing serpents. It was a place dark creatures and wolves would call home, and to Fee it felt like eyes were staring at him from the deepest shadows beneath the mangled canopy. Although there was a good stretch of ground between where they stood and where the thick undergrowth began, he no longer wished to linger upon the border of trees. He glanced at the inquisitor and saw his master still looking into the depths of the wood —as if he could feel the eyes too, but instead of shirking away he chose to challenge their hidden stares. "Do you think it's in there," Fee finally asked, the words catching in the back of his throat.

Blackwood answered without taking his eyes from the tree line. "The children spoke of the lady in the woods, didn't they?"

Fee's heart grew even colder. "Yes. Yes, they did."

Off in the distance, somewhere in the bowels of the woods, the high screech of a bird could be heard. It was sharp and quick, and then the suffocating silence returned. Fee felt some relief when the inquisitor turned his back to the trees and began to make his way down the cobbled street back towards the centre of the village. He followed quickly, still feeling the invisible eyes on the back of his neck as he hurried after Blackwood. "What do we do next?" he asked as he came up on the inquisitor's shoulder.

For the first time since the inquisitor arrived in Westgrave his eyes flashed with a dangerous sense of fortune. The shadow cast by the wide brim of his hat made the look even more intimidating. "We wait," said Blackwood plainly.

8

INTO THE WOODS

The inquisitor and the apprentice waited patiently for the witch to make her move. As the two men made their way through the fog and back towards the inn, Blackwood explained the details of his plan to lure the witch from its lair —and, as he explained, he was sure the she-devil's hideaway was somewhere in the woods outside of Westgrave. Several nights had passed since the visitation on that first evening of Blackwood's arrival in Westgrave. There were no more apparitions or conjuring of shadows in the girl's room. The only things that remained constant as a reminder of the witch's presence was the ever-present fog that suffocated the village and the unnatural sleep that still held Mary Shaw deep within its grasp.

Blackwood's plan was simple. Each night, he would visit Mary Shaw where she lay and perform a simple act of exorcism upon her with the assistance of his inquisitorial coin. By doing so, the inquisitor would slowly break down the hold the witch possessed over the girl. He had done it more times than he could recall during his long years as a hunter of the magic-kind. The coin was imbued with holy litanies, and although it was a powerful divining rod to locate the presence of the *Old Ways* in a limited area, that ability also made it possible for an inquisitor to affect his will upon the nature of whatever magic the coin revealed. Much like drawing the venom from a snake bite, the inquisitor's will worked as a slow acting antidote to the poison. Without fail, Blackwood would enter Mary's room at the same time each evening and perform the exorcism: slowly moving the coin over the girl, from head to toe, whilst focusing his will on the black token and the otherworldly connection it would create when it reacted with the *Old Ways*. Whilst he was in the room, performing the ritual, Fee would be outside, keeping guard at the bedroom door. There had been a growing sense of uneasiness amongst the village-folk as the agents of the Citadel prolonged their stay. For the most part, Mr. Shaw was the source of the ill-feelings towards the two men. Blackwood wanted no interruptions during his efforts to provoke the witch's magic into action. Once the ritual was completed, both Blackwood and Fee would take up positions on the street outside the inn. Blackwood stood at the one end of the village street where he had clear sight of the inn's front door, whilst Fee stood slightly off the cobblestones on the other end so that he could have a vantage point over the smaller kitchen door at the back of the inn. The fog remained unmoving and thick, but the two men positioned themselves well enough so that they maintained sight of each other and the entrances to the inn. The inquisitor's intuition told him that if the witch was to make its move to apprehend her prize—Mary Shaw—she would not risk entering the village itself. Instead, as before, she would exercise its magic and take control of Mary Shaw and lead the girl out of the town and into the safety of the woods; and when this was to happen, they'd be waiting and watching, ready to follow.

Yet, several nights passed and nothing happened. Nightly, Blackwood performed the ritual, slowly chipping away at whatever spell bound Mary Shaw to the witch, channeling his will through the coin in an attempt to coax the sorceress into action. Night after night, the black coin drew no reaction from the girl and no supernatural events occurred. Everything seemed to be quite ordinary. The village folk were beginning to grow anxious. The inquisitor's nightly visits with Mary Shaw, and the absence of any further unnatural occurrences, were beginning to sit uneasily with them. It was strange how quickly the backwater folk could forget what had happened no more than a week ago and even more surprising how quickly Mr. Shaw—who had been in the room during the witch's visitation—had also forgotten what had happened. Or, more likely, forgotten what he'd seen. Blackwood paid no attention to the village folk and their growing unrest with his presence in Westgrave. This was just another investigation, one in a lifetime's worth of such cases, where he'd had to deal with the narrow minds of country folk. He ignored the change in looks from the people in the *Candle and the Cask*. Stares that were once filled with fear and apprehension were now filled with a touch of contempt—anger even. His presence had once set the village folk on edge, but with each passing day, Blackwood could feel that changing. Mornings in the common room were filled with a tense air of frustration. Mr. Shaw still served him and Fee with a simple breakfast, and any other meal they required during the day, but the nervousness of the initial days was gone. Although he feigned ignorance, Blackwood noted each daring look of hatred from the man. Perhaps it was the frustration of a father who was powerless to help his daughter. Certainly, that was a part of it. Another certainty was the fear of a father—the fear of not knowing the fate of a child. And, in the case of Mary Shaw, her current fate contained little hope. The imposing reputation of an inquisitor didn't help in either regard, and, for this, Blackwood forgave the man for his presumptuous behaviour. But if the man's fatherly instincts were to drive him to do something foolish, Blackwood would show him no mercy. There was no excuse for standing against an inquisitor. Not even ignorance was acceptable, let alone the love of a father. He would allow the man to do as he wished, even if that meant walking a dangerous line between expressing his feelings and standing in the way of the Citadel. Mr. Shaw's growing angst toward the inquisitor and his apprentice was beginning to affect the other village folk too, and Blackwood offered them the same treatment. For now, he tolerated them —the witch was his priority—but if it came to it, the people of Westgrave would discover how quickly an inquisitor could bring a village to its knees.

Blackwood spent most of the days in his room, reading through the lexicon of the *Malleus Maleficarum*, going over the accounts of Megen. The question remained unanswered in his mind—why had the witch, intentionally or not, shown him a vision of that particular moment in history? *Killer of children*. The witch's words taunted him. No matter how many times he looked over the details of the story of Megen, he could not understand it. The vision was obscure. Why would she have shown him that particular event? These were the questions which were plaguing his mind since the night of the visitation. *Child-killer*. He refused to believe the obvious implication. It was ludicrous to even consider this witch as the mother of the Seven Sisters. *Impossible*. No *fae* had survived the wars, let alone one so ancient. He pushed such wild ideas from his mind. His brooding was leading him down questionable avenues of thought. Maybe Fee was correct: what if the witch was gathering a coven, stealing newly-become *inherents* from small villages to fill her ranks. It would make sense—after all it was far too dangerous for a witch to operate within the walls of Gotheim. Far too dangerous for any magic-kind for that matter. It had been nearly a century since any form of the *Old Ways* had crossed over the boundaries of the capital. Evil things still occurred with the city, things you'd expect of a place of such size, but the evil was of man, not *fae*. Blackwood considered the geography of the facts. The case of Mary Shaw was not entirely isolated. Three girls had been stolen from nearby villages. The concentration of so many *inherents* in such a small area was also unlikely. Almost unbelievable if he were to consider that these girls would need to be powerful enough in the *Old Ways* to warrant the attention of a witch. *Inherents* capable of small feats such as minor clairvoyance or parlour tricks could be considered common, but individuals born mortal and then to have inherent powers strong enough to put them on par with magic-kind was unbelievable. Those bloodlines had been annihilated during the wars along with all the *fae* bloodlines. They were the exterminated people.

* * *

It was a quiet night, just like those preceding it, when Blackwood stood up from the table in his room and closed the lexicon. He stretched his legs and rubbed the fatigue from his eyes with the ball of his thumb. Distractedly, he placed the *Malleus Maleficarum* back into the worn letter bag and then slipped it into the space between the bed and the small table standing alongside it. Outside his door, he could hear the sound of feet climbing the stairs. He followed the sound as they moved from the wooden floorboards of the landing to the soft carpeted hallway. They came to a halt by his door. It was Fee—come to fetch him for the nightly ritual. Blackwood walked over to the door and took his coat from the hook. The *sharur* was already holstered in his belt and the black coin in his trouser pocket—these two things rarely left his possession, especially during an investigation. He opened the door and as he expected, Fee stood in the dark hallway. His face was soft and relaxed, but his eyes were tight with apprehension. The uneventful nights of the past few days had brought a certain degree of ease to the apprentice, but as the two men moved to carry out Blackwood's plan each night, the nervousness and trepidation returned to trouble the young man's composure. Standing in the poor light of the hallway, Blackwood could see it in Fee's eyes. *Good*, he thought. *I will need you at your best when the time comes.* Even though nothing had happened since his first night in Westgrave, Blackwood was certain it was only a matter of time before something did.

The inquisitor left Fee outside the door of Mary Shaw's bedroom. He was armed with a long knife, concealed in his coat, and a revolver holstered on his belt—the latter only to be use in the most dire of situations. The apprentice's back was the last thing Blackwood saw as he closed the door in its frame, its lock clicking softly into place. He turned and surveyed the room. Nothing had changed since the night before, or the day after the first visitation for that matter. Blackwood had given strict instructions that nothing was to be removed or changed in the room. A bowl of water upon the sitting chair in the corner closest to the window caught his eye. A linen cloth hung over the bowl's lip. The girl's mother must have forgotten to remove it after washing Mary. Blackwood sucked on his teeth with frustration. Village folk could be so trying at times. Apart from the bowl, everything else in the room looked in order. Mary Shaw lay in the same spot, the bedsheet pulled up to her chest, her arms neatly placed to her sides. Her hair was combed in the way he had come to expect, straight down with a side parting. The wounds on her shoulders—those made by the witch's ragged nails—had healed to mere bruises against her fair skin. Even the cuts at the corners of her mouth had nearly disappeared. She seemed peaceful in the grip of that unnatural sleep. Blackwood walked across the room and came to a halt at the foot of the bed. The room was still as warm as the first time he had entered it. The mounds of candles still burnt with the flicker of dozens of flames. A fire crackled in the hearth. The heat from these sources would do little to help the girl—this Blackwood knew. As long as she remained under the influence of the enchantment, her body would not age. It would not change. In fact, it would remain immune to the elements of the natural world. He let the Shaws keep the candles lit and the fire in the hearth burning, not out of sympathy but because fire was the one thing in the natural world most sensitive to the coming of the *Old Ways*—or as the alchemists of the Citadel would put it, *the manifestation of magic*. Blackwood glanced at the dance of the candles and the crackling fire and all seemed to be as it should. He slipped his hand into the trouser pocket that contained the formidable black coin. It was cold against the touch of his skin. With the tip of his finger Blackwood traced the pressing of the Inquisition's sigil upon its surface. *Let us try this again*, he thought.

He walked around the side of the bed and stood over Mary as he had on that first night in Westagrave, and every night thereafter. He pulled the coin from his pocket and positioned it between his fingers so that he could hold it over the girl, like a ward. He then stretched out his arm until his coin hovered over her chest. The inquisitor held the coin there for several long minutes. Nothing happened. There was no stir-

ring in the girl, or in the room. The candles flickered inno-
cently, and no otherworldly force pranced around the
fireplace. The coin remained dormant. Blackwood focused
his will on the coin, gathering it on that black token as if it
were a staging area for an assault, before channeling it into
the girl. He concentrated on that first night, remembering how
Mary Shaw had risen from her slumber in a thrall. The
memories flowed through his mind. Blackwood recalled the
ancient, scraping voice that had spoken the *fae*-tongue. He
remembered the growing shadow from behind the head of the
bed. Still, nothing happened. Despite his efforts, the room
remained undisturbed. Mary continued to sleep peacefully.
Slowly, he moved the coin from her chest to her forehead and
held it there just over the point between her eyes—the point
where the mystics believed the third eye, the eye of the soul,
sat. Again, the inquisitor channelled his will into the black
coin and then focused its power upon the girl. Just like
before, he found no resistance. Mary Shaw remained
unmoving and peaceful, and nothing in the room seemed to
react or shift. Blackwood went deeper into his memories and
drew upon those of that place of nothingness where there had
only been the abyss and himself—and something else. The
scenes of Megen rolled across his mind as he recalled the
annihilation of that town and the immolation of the witches
upon the hilltop. *Nothing*. For a moment, he paused and
thought of his approach—the same approach he had taken
each night—and brooded over the silence from the otherworld. He knew the witch could feel his efforts. Even if it
were the smallest knocking against the walls of the enchantment which held the girl, the witch would feel it. It would be
like the muffled scratching of a rat in the ceiling or like the
whining of a mosquito. *She must feel it*, he thought and so he
pressed on with more resolve. There was one thing both rat

and mosquito did well and that was their relentless persistence, becoming an unending annoyance that eventually broke a person's temper. *All he had to do was the same.* He needed to find the thing that would make the witch lash out against him. He felt with a keenness that he could not shake, that there was something in the vision of Megen that would spark the witch. Blackwood spent several long minutes searching the details of those memories that weren't his and then it finally came to him. He found it. *Of course.* A rare smile touched his face for a moment, too fleeting to truly be there and too weak to touch his eyes. He straightened his arm and strengthened his grip on the coin before delving back into that dark vision. He looked passed the place of nothingness, turning his back on the destruction of the town and pausing at the burning of the women upon the hilltop. The fires burned brightly— the red and orange lapping against the dark night like the forked tongues of dragons. *One. Two. Three ...* Blackwood counted each of them, until his eyes fell upon the girl he recognised. She was the one from the vision. The one he approached with his host-body. The one whose base of kindling he had doused with oil.

The inquisitor focused on the details. In his mind, he could see the oil dripping from her toes before the fire leapt from the kindling and onto her, spreading like a hungry creature of its own. Blackwood concentrated on her face, remembering how it was framed amongst the growing flames that consumed her body. The sweat glistened on her cheeks and brow. Black smoke began to rise from her long dark hair as strands began to catch alight. The most beautifully terrifying aspect of that image was the way the girl's eyes glared down at him, unwavering and fearless, holding the dancing light of fire in their grasp. The words of the witch whispered in the back of his mind: *killer of children. There it was.* Blackwood reinforced his will and channeled his strength into the coin. *Killer of swine*. He yelled those three words from his mind like a provocation, and, with that, the coin between his two fingers went ice cold and took on the weight of a bag full of heavy stones. Blackwood held on with all he could manage. Across the room, the candles flickered and an unfelt gust of wind choked the flames in the fireplace. The light in the room diminished for a blink and a stinging blow rolled across the inquisitor's face. The strike was unexpected, and Blackwood reeled from the pain that spread across his cheek. The black coin slipped from his grasp and tumbled through the air, bouncing off Mary's forehead and landing beside her on the bed. It left an indentation in the sheet far greater than its size could possibly allow for. The candles returned to normal instantly and the fire crackled on as if no otherworldly gust had just disturbed it. Blackwood raised his hand to his cheek and felt a warm welt developing where the invisible blow had landed. Despite the pain, he felt uplifted, and savoured the small victory. He had managed to coax the witch into action. He took the coin from the bed and put it back in his trouser pocket. Mary Shaw remained still but the bruises along her shoulders suddenly seemed more pronounced against her white skin, the cut in the corners of her mouth a touch redder than before and a fine film of perspiration had broken out along her brow. The inquisitor gave her one last brooding stare and then turned to leave the room. *Killer of swine*. The smile returned to his face and lingered there for a moment longer than before.

* * *

Fee followed the inquisitor down the hallway. Blackwood moved quickly, and his long strides seems to devour a number of stairs at once. Those who still remained in the common room frowned at the inquisitor as he crossed the room to the front door. Some stole questioning glances at the mark across his cheek. Blackwood ignored all of them. Once outside, he stood on the porch of the inn, the unending white landscape of fog drifting to the east, but never moving away from Westgrave. The cold air offered slight relief for his cheek. He touched it gently and brushed aside the sharp pain that followed.

Fee came out onto the porch a few moments later and stared at Blackwood's face with the same questioning look as the village folk. "What happened?"

Blackwood simply looked up the cobbled road and then turned to face Fee's curious look. "Let us just say there was a quick exchange of blows," the inquisitor said. A frown creased Fee's forehead and he continued to look at his master with the same questioning stare. Fee's mouth opened slightly, as if he was going to say something, but no words came, and the expression on his face made him seem slightly dim. "It doesn't matter," Blackwood said. "You know where you need to be. And you know what you need to do."

Fee nodded. "Yes I do," he answered and began to make his way off the porch, walking toward his lookout point by the rear door of the inn. "Another night of waiting in the cold," he said jokingly, trying to make light of the grim weather and the serene look upon the inquisitor's face.

The young man's attempt at humour was short-lived as Blackwood's dark eyes followed him down the porch. "I have a feeling tonight will be different," he said softly to himself, Fee already out of earshot.

The inquisitor walked across the street to the corner of the stone building opposite the inn. It was the sole merchant store in Westgrave, and although the fog and darkness of night concealed it well, it was much like the hundreds of small village merchant stores he had seen before. A small awning hung over its front and a bench stood beneath each window that flanked the door. The wide windows were dark now, but during the day the merchant kept lanterns burning to ward off the gloom of the unnatural weather. Blackwood leaned against the wall of the store and, from the dark shadows beneath the awning, he looked up at the inn. Even though the benches offered a bit of comfort in the cold, dreary night, the inquisitor would not sit—not for the remainder of his vigil. Off in the distance, despite the broiling fog, he could make out the faint outline of Fee keeping his own watch higher up the street. The inn loomed ahead, its bulk standing against the floating mist like a bulwark. The lights from the common room glowed warmly in the darkness of the night, but it was the single lit window on the second floor that kept Blackwood's attention. Mary Shaw's room. After the visitation, the inn had emptied out, leaving the inquisitor and his apprentice as the only occupants of the establishment. *Tonight will be different*. He could feel it. The sharpened intuition of an inquisitor hummed with certainty. He had managed to coax the witch into action after the long nights of silence. The absence of the witch's magic over the last few days may have fooled the village folk into a false sense of comfort and belief that she had moved on, but Blackwood knew better. Mary Shaw's unchanging condition, and the persistent weather were clear indications that the witch's influence was still at hand. *Yes, something would happen tonight*. He could feel it in his bones.

* * *

Time passed slowly at first. The minutes carrying into hours,

the hours lingering like the smothering fog until the passing
of time became as indistinct as the gloom over Westgrave.
The night had moved into its final quarter, those darkest
hours of its reign over the world when the shadows were
deepest and all the kingdoms of night-crawlers and nocturnal
creatures fulfilled their business upon the land. The silence
was monotonous. The common room of the inn was now
dark, the last lanterns extinguished some time ago, and even
the light from the fire in the hearth could no longer be seen
from outside— although its embers still glowed a dark
crimson amongst the ashes of the exhausted wood. The
window of Mary Shaw's bedroom remained aglow, the only
beacon of light against the darkness of the night. Down the
road, toward the train station, the line of lamps which had led
Blackwood into the village had also been extinguished some
time ago. Through the darkness, Blackwood's sharp eyes
could still make out the dim figure of his apprentice in the
near distance. He commended the man's dedication and fortitude, despite his lacking in some important aspects of what
would complete him as an inquisitor. Yet, Fee was young and
there was still time until he would have to take the rites of an
inquisitor. *Once hardened he would make a fine* inquisitor,
Blackwood thought. *Perhaps not the greatest, but well worth
the title.*

Something shifted against the only light in the darkness
and the inquisitor's eyes darted from the silhouette of his
apprentice to the window of Mary Shaw's bedroom with
catlike speed. A shadow, slim and upright, passed behind the
drawn curtains. *Mary.* The inquisitor straightened against the
wall of the merchant store, the cold which had gathered in his
muscles quickly falling away, and stepped to the edge of the
deep shadow of the awning. Another shadow passed behind
the curtain, trailing closely behind the first with hands

stretched out, as if guiding the former. As it passed before the window, it appeared bent and crooked against the light of the room. A shiver ran down the inquisitor's back. Blackwood pursed his lips and let out a short but sharp whistle. In the distance, Fee's silhouette shifted in the fog. Out in the darkness of the night, the inquisitor's whistle was met by the loud shrill call of a bird. Another shiver crawled down Blackwood's arms, his sense of danger heightening. *No birds were awake at this dark hour*. He remained still, not daring to move in case he jeopardised his place of hiding beneath the awning.

The inn door creaked but did not open. Blackwood's eyes burnt through the darkness and watched carefully, each second now seeming to stretch out, and it was in moments like this that he could imagine a predator's perception of time change as it moved into the final act of killing. The door moved outward, and then swung back into position, the sound of wood against wood clanking through the silence. Finally, the door opened wide enough and the slim, pale form of Mary Shaw appeared on the porch of the inn.

She stood there for a short moment, as if taking in her surroundings, and then descended onto the cobbled street and began walking up toward the woods. Blackwood did not move as he watched the fog consume the girl from sight. Only once she was entirely hidden did he leap from below the awning and follow her up the street. Up ahead he could see the shape of Fee move too, approaching from the side to meet him. The apprentice came up on his right shoulder and, even in the darkness, Blackwood could see the tension plastered on Fee's face. "Now the hunt begins," Blackwood whispered, and the young man forced a nervous smile.

The two men followed from a safe distance, keeping pace with the girl just enough to keep the shape of her waif-like form in sight. The fog shifted on either side of them and Blackwood allowed experience to take hold of him. He controlled the length of his strides so as not to let the growing heat of the hunt overcome him. Fee followed a step behind. "Stay close," the inquisitor whispered over his shoulder. "There's no knowing what snares the witch has laid for us in this murk." Fee gave no answer and the inquisitor took that as a sign of the young man's understanding.

Into the white they strode, trailing the girl, her bare feet making no sound on the cobbled street. The inquisitor and apprentice walked as silently, carefully placing each step so as not to have a misplaced boot scratch against the stone beneath them. The girl walked in a daze, her back upright and her palms slightly turned open before her, as if she were approaching a doorway. The dark shapes of houses passed on either side of the street—the village of Westgrave caught deeply in the spell of the night. Darker shapes began to appear through the murk. Blackwood and Fee knew those obscure spectres to be the tree line of the woods. Soon the gnarled and ominous keepers of that wooded land would appear through the fog and the line between civilisation and wilderness would be drawn. The fog began to darken, the otherworldly white changing into a dense smog as the shadow of the looming woods began to enforce itself. Unperturbed by the darkness, Mary Shaw walked into the haze and disappeared from sight. It was then that Blackwood knew she had passed over the dividing line and entered the woods that surrounded Westgrave. He hastened his steps, still careful not to make any unwanted sound that may draw the girl's attention to her rear, or worse, call the attention of any creatures under the domain of the witch to their presence.

The inquisitor paused at the edge of the woods, Fee coming up on his shoulder, the young man's breath a slight pant in the silence. It was nothing but nerves, but Blackwood could not risk even the slightest sound. "Steady yourself, Fee," he whispered in a voice that was barely audible. Before them, the wall of trees stretched into the gloom on either side. In the darkness of the night, the bulging trunks and twisted branches seemed more menacing. Deep shadows, blacker than the night, lurked beneath the canopy and the woods' harbingers seemed to challenge the men's resolve. Again, somewhere in the unknown depths of the night, the nocturnal cry of some bird disturbed the blanket of silence. In reply to the bird's call of doom, Blackwood reached behind him and withdrew the polished handle of the *sharur* and held it, at the ready, at his side. He could feel the eyes of his apprentice upon the horrible weapon and Blackwood turned to look at Fee from beneath the brim of his hat. "Stay close," he whispered again. "For into the darkness we now go, and what evil we find there, we will surely face head on."

With those words, Blackwood turned and took the first step over the dividing line into the woods.

Fee unsheathed his long dagger with one hand and pulled the revolver out of its holster with the other. He took one deep breath and followed his master.

9

THE WITCH OF WESTGRAVE

The fog seemed to recede as the men stalked through the woods. The thick banks of fog dissipated beneath the canopy, revealing a chaotic spider web of entangled branches overhead. At one point it dropped to waist height and then diminished to a blanket of mist that swirled around the men's ankles and hugged the protruding tree roots and underbrush. The air was still here, the thickness of the trees preventing the invasion of any fresh air, and the heavy smell of a forest— that of decay and growth—filled the men's nostrils. There was a strange twilight within the woods. Darkness mixed with the rich tones of the old trees and a strange green umbra hung over the place like a veil. With the fog no longer all encompassing, Mary Shaw was far more visible. She wandered through the woods, her hands still frozen in that gesture of offering and her back in an upright position as if a stick had slid down the back of her nightgown. Her long, dark hair cascaded down to her lower back, unmoving in the still air of the woods. She moved with ease, navigating the treacherous forest floor, her bare feet stepping over reaching roots and spiteful weeds, and she avoided the touch of any branch or leaf with uncanny agility. Blackwood noticed the absence of tracks in the wake of her path, not even the hint of a single footprint, or the snap of a branch, or the remains of a crushed leaf. It was as if her passage through the woods were an illusion —as if she was not really there. The inquisitor immediately discarded the idea that he was following a spectre as a ludicrous notion. Such thoughts were unwelcome in such a place, where the ancient breath of the trees played their games with the mind, and the schemes of a witch lurked maliciously in the twilight shadows.

The two men stepped carefully, weaving around wide tree trunks, moving over twisted roots and avoiding any brush that would give away their position with the unwanted sound of a broken branch. They moved deeper into the woods, taking cover from tree to tree as they followed Mary Shaw. She appeared as a virgin forest nymph, her white nightgown seeming incorporeal amongst the shadows and bent trees. Blackwood still held the *sharur* in his one hand, and, in the other, he now held the black coin. Since he and Fee had entered the woods, the coin had begun to pull at his trouser pocket as it gained weight against the presence of the *Old Ways*. The further they moved into the dark forest, the colder the coin grew and the heavier it became. For now, it was no heavier than a pouch of silver coins. Blackwood kept his fist closed around it, not risking dropping it into the undergrowth that covered the ground. Fee followed in the footsteps of the inquisitor, dagger and revolver at the ready. He had come to question the efficiency of his weapons in their current situation. On either side, the forest disappeared into the horizonless distance, trees becoming dark shapes and shadows until all that could be seen was the strange green twilight that hung over the place. Anything could be lurking out there or, worse, stalking them from those shadows. *What was a long dagger and four-shot revolver going to do against whatever waited for them? Especially when they were in the process of hunting a witch.* The *sharur* in the hand of the inquisitor gave Fee much relief though. He'd not seen it in use before, but he'd read about it from the texts in the Citadel library and had heard the stories of what it could do. Mercy be with whatever came charging out of the thickets of the underbrush and had to face the *sharur.* If anything, his simple dagger and pistol would be used to dispatch whatever the inquisitor's weapon did not annihilate completely. Nevertheless, he tightened his grip on the handle of the dagger and kept his finger close to the pistol trigger. Whatever would happen, he would be ready.

Onward the three went through the forest—the girl, ghostly in her white gown, leading the way and the two men, ready for whatever evil may fall upon them, following behind. It seemed like they would carry on walking for what was left of the night when the unending, forest ahead began to change. The night-bird cried again, this time closer than ever before, its cry loud and sharp. Blackwood paused and took cover in the bowl formed by two large twisting roots of an ancient, bulbous tree. Fee slipped into the natural depression, coming to rest in an awkward squat alongside his master. Mary Shaw stopped too. Ahead of her the trees were less dense, the great earthly pillars more widespread, giving way to a mound protruding from the ground. A wide mouth stretched across the front of the mound and within it there was only darkness. *A cave.* Blackwood leaned against the fat root in front of him, crossing his arms, as he surveyed the area. Once, the cave must have been a rough rocky hump jutting out from the ground, but now it was completely overrun by the undergrowth of the forest. Thick clumps of ferns and young saplings whose roots had managed to find a foothold amongst the crags had come to cover the rock, and now it looked like a massive burial mound, reclaimed by nature. Mary Shaw stood before it and slowly stretched out her arms, palms turned to the sky, and offered herself to the cave. Again, the night-bird crowed as the girl began to approach the mouth of the cave. Blackwood scanned the higher branches of the towering trees surrounding the cave but could not see the night-bird. The inquisitor simply watched as the girl disappeared into the black entrance of the cave.

At his side the inquisitor could sense Fee's restlessness. "We should follow," the apprentice whispered. By now, he too had leaned forward, using the large root as a leaning post —both dagger and pistol hanging listlessly over its wide berth.

Blackwood remained quiet. His attention was focused on the mouth of the cave and the high branches around it. It was common for magic-kind to use winged creatures as their spies, and he was not going to allow a night-bird to announce their arrival. He waited for another few long moments, peering into the mangled canopy, trying to notice any movement amongst the still branches. "Just wait," he replied.

Fee followed the inquisitor's eyes into the canopy and mimicked his master. Yet there was no movement. There were no signs of the night-bird in the trees around the cave. "We're going to lose Mary to the darkness of the cave if we don't follow," he persisted.

Still staring into the canopy, Blackwood gritted his teeth. Fee was right. There was only so much longer they could wait, before the girl's path into the cave became unknown. He tightened his fist around the black coin. *There were, of course, other ways to track the girl*. Yet, focusing his willpower through the coin to track the trail of magic possessing the girl would leave him vulnerable to attack, and, although he had confidence in his apprentice, Fee's recent hesitations in their confrontation with the witch didn't leave him with a sense of security. He had to make a decision. Just as he was about to vault over the root that concealed them, Fee grabbed his arm.

"There," the apprentice called, his voice barely a whisper. With the tip of the dagger, Fee pointed at a feeble tree, withered and struggling for life, far below the line of branches Blackwood had been surveying. Upon one of the tree's weakest branches sat an ominous bird, gaunt and ghastly, the colour of midnight.

Blackwood nodded. *How clever,* he thought, and just like that, the winged dirge let off another shriek and took off from the branch. Its tattered wings spreading wide, the bird flew off into the darkness of the forest.

Fee glanced nervously at Blackwood.

There was no more time to waste. The inquisitor leapt out of the ditch and strode toward the mouth of the cave.

Fee scrambled after him. "Do you think it saw us," he called with a hushed voice.

"I don't think so," Blackwood answered darkly. Despite his reply, in his secret heart, something was beginning to gnaw at him, and that was the alarming notion that the witch was aware of their presence, even before they had entered the forest. If that was the case, he was unsure what they would face in the darkness of the cave. It was too late though. He tightened his grip around the *sharur* and pressed on, his eyes set on the mouth of the cave.

* * *

Blackwood and Fee stared blindly down the throat of the

cave. The air was surprisingly fresh and lacked the smell of long-deceased carcasses and animal waste that they had expected. The darkness was stubborn here, and no matter how hard they stared into its maw, neither one of them could make out anything distinct. This was dangerous, but the inquisitor kept his concerns to himself. "Are you ready?"

Fee swallowed hard and answered with the only word he could, "Yes."

The two men strode into the cave, leaving behind the murky twilight of the forest. The way into the cave quickly began to slope downward into the earth and what little light came from outside vanished. The unspoilt air turned quickly too, and a foul stifling stench began to meet them from whatever depths the cave reached. They moved silently, following the underground passage as it meandered from side to side. Slowly, their eyes began to adjust to the darkness and they could make out smaller passageways breaking off from the main tunnel, but Blackwood held their course and pushed on into the blackness. They followed the lines of the cave walls as their only corporeal guide. Blackwood still held onto the black coin in his hand, and, with every step, it gained another pinch of weight. As long as it continued to do so, he knew they were moving in the right direction. The foulness of the air worsened, thickening with each breath. The inquisitor pushed on, following the slow arc of the passageway as it veered left, and Fee walked quietly behind. The darkness seemed to lessen as they pressed on, and Blackwood glanced over his shoulder to look at Fee. For the first time since entering the cave and leaving the dismal twilight of the woods behind, Blackwood could make out the features of Fee's face. *The darkness was fading.* As they followed the bend in the passageway, dim light—a failing yellow glow— flickered in the distance. It was too far to know its source, and the inquisitor slowed his paced. Despite the underground cold, sweat gathered between his shoulder blades and trickled down his back. Beneath his coat and waistcoat, he could feel his shirt cling to is body.

"What is it?" Fee asked.

"I don't know," Blackwood answered. He kept his eyes fixed on the passage and the light at its end.

"And that on the walls?" the apprentice asked again.

Blackwood peered through the darkness and saw white tufts of silken webs springing from the cracks in the rock walls. "Spiders," the inquisitor said, his voice hard against the silence.

"It looks like fur." Fee approached the wall to his right to examine the strange, glassy tufts and saw bulbous spiders scurrying from the webs, abandoning their haunts to avoid his prying eyes.

The glow at the end of the passageway faltered. Shapes shifted across the light, moving from side to side, slowly advancing on where they stood. Fee noticed the movement too and stood frozen against the wall. He tried to raise his pistol in the direction of the moving shapes. Something was wrong. His hand would not move. He tried to raise the pistol again, but still it would not move to his command. Fee looked down at the hand that held the revolver and saw entangling threads reaching from one of the tufts of web, wrapping themselves around his hand, ensnaring it in place. He tried to leap away but his feet were also rooted to the ground. Threads of web enclosed around his boots and held him where he stood. Panic washed over his body. The wall of spider webs was growing as tufts of webs reached out for him, thousands of searching ends building bridges through the air. A heaving mass of spiders gathered along the base of each reaching tuft and a vanguard of eight-legged horrors were already making the first crossings over the tenuous bridges to his hand and feet. "Blackwood," he cried, still trying to pull free from the webs' clutches.

Blackwood turned from the approaching shapes and saw Fee wrestle against what seemed to be a giant claw made of spider webs that reached out from the cave wall. In a blurring series of movements, the inquisitor whirled the *sharur* over his head and sent forth a lashing whip of scaled blades from the polished handle. The whip cut through the webs on Fee's arm. Blackwood drew it back to send another sweeping lash across the apprentice's feet but something with the force of a hammer knocked into his chest, sending him stumbling backward, off his feet. Crouching where he had just been standing was a hideous form, covered in dirt and all other means of filth. Long hair, tangled in thick clumps, stuck out in all directions making a feral crown around the creature's face. It squatted on its haunches, swaying from left to right, its arms resting on its knees as it watched the inquisitor get back to his feet. It let out a garbled moan and then scurried back into the darkness of the passageway. The inquisitor positioned himself, taking the stance to fight, and the slow crackle of magic imbued in the *sharur* filled the passageway as the bladed whip withdrew back into the polished handle.

"Master," Fee called out again, this time the alarm in his voice more dire than before. The apprentice had managed to keep his pistol-hand free from the webs, but the tendrils of webs continued to wrap themselves around him. A swarm of spiders advanced over the silken bridges, hungry to deliver their poisonous bites. Yet, it was not the growing snare of webs or the creeping advance of the spiders that seemed to alarm Fee. He raised the four-shot revolver and fired a single shot down the dark passage.

The shot reverberated with deafening thunder against the

cave walls, and the inquisitor could feel its force against his
chest in the confines of the underground place. Blackwood
looked down the passage and saw three figures stalking the
sides of the passageway with inhuman speed. One scurried
along the wall to the left, seemingly covering several feet
with each bound. On the right, another sped toward their
position on foot, and, down the centre, something crept low
and slower than the other two. Fee fired another shot, the
round ricocheting harmlessly from a cave wall in the
distance. Burnt gunpowder filled the cave with its acrid
smoke and the calamity of the second shot rang in Blackwood's ears. "Stop firing," he ordered as he watched the three
assailants continue unimpeded by the threat of a gun.
Shooting wildly into the darkness was doing neither of them
any good. He widened his stance and willed the *sharur* into
the form of a longsword. The broad blade crackled into existence as the magic captured in the polished handle came
alive.

From the left a dark figure lunged from darkness,
becoming visible at the very last moment, but Blackwood had
taken his stance and was prepared, even though he caught the
attack at the very last moment. He turned on the balls of his
feet and moved out of the path of the intended strike. Midway
between his manoeuvre he parried with a strike of his own.
He tracked the line of the attacker's charge and brought the
long blade of the *sharur* down across its path in a single
swooping arc. The *sharur*'s blade glided through the point
where neck met shoulder, and for a moment he felt the resistance of flesh and bone against the blade before it dismem-
bered head from body.

Blackwood regained his stance as quickly as he had
dodged the charge and prepared himself for the next attack.
The other two shapes shifted in the darkness, their advance

halted by the sudden dispatching of their companion. Against the wall, Fee still struggled to pull free from the entangling webs. The white threads had already climbed up his legs, encasing him in a waist-high cocoon. Other webs were beginning to reach down from the ceiling, more spiders swarming around the ends of those advancing threads. Fee swept his dagger across the surface, slicing and sweeping waves of spiders from his legs, but the webs regenerated quicker than he could cut through them. Soon the attack from the top would enclose him completely. Time was running out for the young apprentice and Blackwood needed to do something to save Fee's life. He stepped toward Fee and swung the *sharur* at the webs threatening from the passageway ceiling. As the *sharur* travelled through the air, by the will of the inquisitor, the long sword transformed back into a bladed whip and cut through the growing curtain of spiderwebs. The lacerated tendrils, heavy with clinging spiders, rained down upon Fee and the apprentice quickly turned his attention to taking care of the eight-legged terrors before the agony of a thousand bites overwhelmed him. He could feel the minute denizens of the darkness swarm beneath his clothes, their fangs delivering needle-like servings of pain. One bite was bearable, but the tide that washed over his body felt like a firestorm.

A blast, like a moving fist of air, rammed into Blackwood's side, toppling him over onto the hard ground. His shoulder took much of the fall and he could hear the shoulder of his coat tear against the rough stone. Almost immediately one of the creatures came bounding out of the darkness at him, its wild mane of hair congealed with filth and wreathed with twigs and leaves. The face that looked at him was nightmarish. Blank white eyes stared from a young face turned grotesque, and a dried waterfall of blood and guts—made of rodents and small woodland creatures—decorated its chin like warpaint. The creature gargled something incoherent between its panting breath, and another blast of hardened air shot from its outstretched hands. Blackwood held the *sharur* up against the spell and channelled his willpower into its handle, directing his resolve toward the charging creature. The *sharur* acted as an amplifier for his resolve, turning it into an anathema for whatever magic he faced. There was a loud clap as his willpower cut through the blast of air, amputating it from its source of power. Nothing more than a strong wind whipped across Blackwood's face and the charging creature hissed in anger. Blackwood rolled onto one knee and lunged with the *sharur*, its form turning at his command from the whip into a spear, its long-reaching point whistling through the air, seeking the throat of the hideous creature. But the thing that charged at him moved with an inhuman agility, shifting from one spot to another, its movements a blur. The fiend ducked beneath the spear and rushed the inquisitor. But Blackwood's experience with the weapon was too great, and, as quickly as the spear had struck from the tip of the polished handle, it retracted, stopping short of a short sword. As the creature closed the ground between them, the inquisitor leapt forward in a counter-attack and lashed at the fiend's hideous snarl. Again, it moved too quickly and his eyes struggled to follow it completely. It evaded the counter-attack and spun upon its feet, taking Blackwood's flank. A sharp pain ripped across his side and he staggered forward as the momentum of his counter-strike was foiled. He glanced down to see his coat in tatters and his waistcoat split open. Fine drops of blood seeped through the mesh of armour that lined his waistcoat. *Lucky*, he thought. If not for the mesh, the strike would have disembowelled him. Blackwood turned to face his attacker which was already beginning to circle him, its chest heaving heavily beneath ragged garments, its pale eyes glimmering in the darkness. Blackwood noticed the human-like fingers distended into claws hanging at the creature's sides. A blow to an unguarded area from one those hands would surely mean the end of him. He shaped the *sharur* into a sword and began to move in a counter direction, waiting for the next charge.

* * *

Fee brushed the last remnants of the webs from his shoulders. He could feel the cocoon that encased the lower half of his body constrict his legs and slowly overtake his stomach. Above him the webs cut by Blackwood were already regenerating. Spiders crawled all over him and he could feel the heat of countless bites spread across his hands and neck. Some had even managed to get in beneath his collar and he could feel the small horrors crawl over his skin, biting as they went. A lightheadedness was beginning to encroach on his mind and his tongue stuck to the dry roof of his mouth. *Poison.* He needed to do something to change his situation. In the darkness he could see Blackwood in combat with one of the remaining creatures. One was dead on the ground already, its head lying lifelessly against the bloody heap of the body it was once attached to, but the one his master now faced had managed to land a successful blow with one of its hideously taloned hands. The thing moved too quickly for him to follow, and he was amazed at how the inquisitor managed to stand his ground against its incessant attacks. Fee gritted his teeth and slipped the blade of his dagger down the front of his shirt, beginning to cut away at the webs that held him in place. He ignored the spiders trawling his skin and pushed through the weariness that was beginning to overcome him. The dagger cut through the webs easily enough and his spirit rose with hope until an unclean hand grabbed his wrist and pulled the dagger away from the webs. He looked up and was met by a terrifying face—a mask of something turned feral, living on what was found in the wilderness. Blank, white eyes glared at him and a foul stench of filth filled his nostrils. Fear took hold of him and, although he could not bear to look upon the face that stood mere inches from his own, Fee could not find the will to look away. There was something human beneath the hideousness of the face—something young, once innocent. Strands of red hair hung from the tattered mess upon the creature's head and it seemed to be wearing a dress —torn and discoloured but, yes, a dress. He was sure of it. *It can't be*. He looked upon the creature with disbelief and tried to pull his hand free from its grasp, but it tightened its hold and he yelled out in pain. His wrist felt like it was cracking. Pain seared up his forearm and Fee clenched his jaw. The creature looked at him quizzically, its head cocked to the side in the same way a cat looks at its prey and decides if it's worth playing with or whether to give it a quick death. In the moment it paused to study him, its face softened by curiosity, the creature resembled a girl rather than some awful thing from the darkness. He was struck with disbelief again. *Surely not*. Once more, Fee tried to free his hand but the thing twisted it, and the pain shot through his bones and into his shoulder. He could nothing but let out another yell. This seemed to give the thing pleasure and it pulled on his arm again. Fee bit on his lip and winced, refusing to give the creature any satisfaction from his suffering. Slowly, its mouth opened, and continued to do so until it was distended beyond any human possibility. Black and hollow, with the foul stench of rotting earth, the mouth blew into his face with a hot sigh. In an instant, Fee was reminded of Mary Shaw's gawping maw in *The Candle and Cask's* common room and her bedroom— and then the apprentice was sure. This was not some devil from a nightmare, but one of the missing girls from the other towns.

* * *

The girl moved her face closer to his, her mouth opening even wider as the distance between them narrowed. Blood trickled from the cuts where the corners of her lips had torn open. From deep within her throat came the rattling flutter of wings, like the thunder of a thousand chitinous wings, rasping and hissing against one another. Glistening carapaces crawled in the back of her throat in one giant heaving mass and the noise burrowed into Fee's ears. The fetid smell worsened, and Fee knew death approached from the depths of the girl's stretched mouth. The hot air of the girl's breath moistened Fee's face, and he held his breath against the terrible doom it brought. *Emperor, have mercy on my soul*, he prayed. He clenched his eyes and turned his face away. Spiders scurried all over him, webs entangling his entire body, and it was a matter of seconds before his death crawled from the girl's mouth. In a moment of clarity, just before he was sure of his demise, calm washed over Fee and the fear which had paralysed him appeared to vanish. He suddenly remembered the revolver in his other hand. *Emperor, have mercy on my soul*. The darkness between his face and the girl's was washed in a blinding flash of white light and the thick smoke of burnt gunpowder filled the air. Fee opened his eyes, his ears ringing with the concussion of the shot, but before him blue smoke rose from the girl's open mouth and ears. The white film in her eyes disappeared and revealed the dark green eyes of a young woman. Fee looked down at the pistol now in his hand beneath her chin and watched as a thin line of blood began to drip onto his hand. The girl's grip on his wrist loosened and she offered him a confused stare as if she could not understand where she was or what was happening. All at once, she collapsed to the ground, dead in the cold dark of the underground.

* * *

Blackwood moved to the left, his breathing elevated and his senses tuned to the pace of the fight. The sting of the wound at his side was nothing more than an irritant and did nothing to hinder his ability to keep the creature at bay. They had gone several rounds, each time the creature rushing him at its bestial speed, talon-like hands whirling through the air. Although the creature was fast, so incredibly quick, it had little knowledge of combat and manoeuvres. It simply charged, stringing together one chaotic action after the other, hoping its speed would be enough to overcome the inquisitor. Yet skill always triumphed, and if not skill, then luck. From the corner of his eye Blackwood could see Fee battling against the third creature in what looked to be a close quarter grapple. There was nothing he could do for his apprentice, not until he dispatched the fiend before him. He could only hope that Fee would be resourceful enough to take his fate into his own hands. The creature began to pace to the right, following Blackwood's movement, remaining in front of him at all times. Its hands began to turn in circular motions, as if it were moulding an invisible ball out of the air. Twisting pillars of smoke and spark began take form within the invisible globe, churning in all directions, until a solid orb of ash and fire swirled between the fiend's moving hands. Blackwood had never seen anything like it before, but he knew what he faced. A spell of some kind, an orb of fire conjured from the power of the *Old Ways*. He took hold of the *sharur* in both his hands and held it before him like a conductor rod, preparing for the onslaught of the spell. Like before, he channeled his willpower into the handle and, in a matter of moments, he could feel the might of his resolve amplify, forming a barrier between himself and the creature. He glanced down and noticed how the creature's feet had changed stance, it too preparing for its next move. Blackwood could gauge its intentions as clear as the day's light. It would rush him again as soon as it unleashed the orb, most probably in a gambit to take him off-guard while he focused his willpower against the power of the spell. It was a clever move, but he would be prepared for it. He waited for the fiend to initiate the attack, watching as it continued to caress the orb of fire between its palms. The building tension was suddenly broken by a deafening clap that filled the dark passageway. Blackwood glanced at the source of the thunder and saw the creature before Fee collapse to the ground, the back of its head a mangled mess of shattered bone and tissue, blue smoke rising from the crater left by the exit of a bullet.

"It's them," Fee yelled, his face pale and drawn in the darkness. "It's the missing girls," he cried again.

Blackwood looked back at the creature in front of him and saw the momentary look of fear and confusion on its face before the horrible feral quality returned—and in that moment the inquisitor saw the girl-like qualities hidden beneath the layers of filth and congealed blood. He could almost visualise the haggard crown of hair combed neatly and tied in place with ribbons chosen by a caring mother. But the moment passed quickly and, before any resemblance of mercy could settle in his mind, Blackwood was on the move. The twisted girl still looked at her fallen companion, her white eyes focused on the heaped body. Blackwood needed no other invitation. He closed the ground between them in three long strides and brought the blade down on the girl's hands in one fell sweep. Her hands toppled from the ends of her wrists, fine fountains of blood spraying into the dank air. The orb of fire blinked twice and then vanished from existence. Before the tormented girl could let out a cry of pain, Blackwood brought the *sharur* back in a reverse cut and severed the girl's head from her shoulders. Silence returned to the passageway.

* * *

The inquisitor wasted no time and hurried to his apprentice. Both of them made quick work of the webs that still held Fee to the ground, but already they could see that they had stopped growing. Even the spiders had retreated back into the darkness. Fee's first steps of freedom were stumbling movements, but he quickly gained his composure despite the increasing lightheadedness. All across his hands and neck, and some way down his chest and back, he could feel the spider bites burn with poison. Blackwood turned and began to examine the three bodies sprawled in the darkness. Whatever magic possessed the girls was already receding back into the otherworld. And the haggard and twisted aspect on the now dead faces had faded away, revealing smooth complexions of gentle skin while the long talons had shrunk into the delicate hands of young girls. By the look of it, the girls had been living like animals of the wild—their dresses were torn and ruined and their feet nearly black with dirt.

What schemes of evil are at work here, Blackwood asked himself. Only moments earlier, the three dead girls were something other—hideous thralls acting at the will of the witch.

Fee's assumption of a coven was seeming more plausible. Had they just killed the first initiates of a new enclave of witches? Blackwood looked upon the dead, with that thought in the forefront of his mind, and felt little for those he and Fee had killed. He looked toward the glowing light at the end of the passageway and his thoughts turned to Mary Shaw. This was her fate—to become a wretched she-devil, bent to the command of a witch. Perhaps it was already too late to save her— if that had ever been an option. She had been touched by the *Old Ways*—to what degree was still unknown—but it was impossible that anyone touched by magic would escape the judgement of the Citadel. The light at the end of cave flickered with movement, and Blackwood knew that was where they would meet their prey. He was sure of it. Why else would the witch have sent her thralls to meet them? He tightened his grip around the handle of the *sharur* and stepped toward the light. Fee joined at his side, his face drawn but resolute, and Blackwood felt encouraged by his apprentice's strength.

They strode into the failing darkness, leaving the bodies of the dead girls behind them. The smell of dank earth and decay grew stronger as they approached what seemed to be a chamber. A voice whispered in the back of Blackwood's mind: *Killer of children*. It was a gentle, soothing voice—the voice of a seductress.

"There's a voice in my head," Fee whispered.

Blackwood looked at the young man and nodded. "As in mine."

"She's telling me impossible things. Master, she's promising me things," Fee's voice trembled as he spoke.

"She's lying to you," the inquisitor growled. "Ignore her deceits. Nothing she offers you is real. Anything the witch says or promises you will only lead to death."

Killer of children, the soothing voice uttered in his mind again.

The entrance to the chamber grew nearer and with every step toward it, Blackwood gathered his strength against the fear of what awaited them in that flickering light. He clenched the coin in his hand until he could feel its edges cut into his skin. The black token and *sharur* were keeping the witch from his mind, holding her whispers at bay, but he could see the strain on Fee's face. The apprentice was fighting against the intrusion of his mind, but it was taking its toll on him. Blackwood would offer him the black coin, even the *sharur*, if he could. But the boy had no training with the token and it would offer him no aid, and the hallowed weapon would more than likely kill him before it bent to his will. A *sharur* was bound to a single inquisitor. That is how it had always been. Again, he felt powerless to help Fee and it would be up to the boy himself to determine his fate. The inquisitor could not fight the battle in Fee's mind on the boy's behalf.

The inquisitor and his apprentice walked into the pool of light emanating from the entrance of the chamber. Blackwood looked at Fee with those hard, black eyes, "Whatever happens in there, Fee, remember who you are. Remember your name. Remember that you are an apprentice of the Citadel, initiate of the Inquisition. Do not give into any illusions or temptations you may face. The witch is a master of deception. I will do what I can to make this swift."

Sweat beaded on Fee's face. Spider bites, swollen and red, pocked his neck and his eyes were glassy. "I can feel her in every thought," he stuttered.

"As long as they are your thoughts Fee, you're winning the battle," Blackwood said, and with that, he stepped into the chamber at the end of the passageway.

The chamber looked like a sepulchre. Hundreds of black dragon candles, conjoined by rivulets of melted wax, formed steep slopes along the curved walls. It was said that the flame of a dragon candle would never die as long as the one who lit it still drew breath—a living bond between flame and soul. The *fae* had found ways to manipulate that bond, drawing on the energy of the eternal flame to cast powerful magic. Blackwood had never witnessed the ruin brought on by the power pulled from a dragon candle before, but he'd read about the everlasting curses bound to these wax artefacts. He gazed upon the number amassed in the chamber with disbelief. They were rare artefacts and to see so many in one place was unheard of. Odd figures of bone and branches hung from rough string, cluttering the stone ceiling. A mural, faded to near nothingness and painted from natural pigments, still survived on the far wall—the last remnant of an ancient shrine.

Mary Shaw stood in front of a large mound of dragon candles, her palms open to the flames, her back to the entrance of the chamber and the two men.

"So enters the killer of children and his loyal pup," a woman's voice slowly purred.

The witch sat in a circle of dragon candles in the centre of the chamber. She was bare down to the waist and her sun-kissed skin glistened in the candlelight. Her back arched as she traced foreign shapes in the sand with a bone talon. Blackwood could not avert his eyes from the witch and, even though she still looked down at the symbols drawn in the sand, he could feel her gaze burrow into him. Fee took a step toward her and Blackwood stretched out his arm and barred Fee from taking another step. "Stop Fee," he ordered.

The witch twisted the talon through the soil, drawing one last rune beside the others and pausing, as if contemplating what she had written, before looking at Blackwood. She was unlike the terrible image Fee had described. There was no scaled face of a hag, twisted and corrupted by age and black magic. Instead, a young face, strikingly beautiful, looked upon him. Thick black hair, matted with leaves and twigs, fell past her shoulders and covered her naked breasts. Upon her brow sat a crown of white feathers, a stark contrast against her smokey hair. A band of charcoal was painted across her eyes, and her lips, frighteningly alluring, were covered with the same black pigment. Her golden eyes moved from Blackwood to Fee and she smiled, revealing sick black teeth behind those tempting lips. "Have you come to kill another one of my children, hunter?" the witch asked, her eyes still fixed on Fee.

"No, I've come to kill you," Blackwood declared. The blade of a longsword formed from the polished handle of the *sharur* and the inquisitor stepped in front of his apprentice.

An insidious laugh emanated from the back of the witch's throat, an unnatural laugh that haunted her words and seemed to come from her black soul. "Don't insult me," she hissed. "You and a dozen of your kind could not bring me down. As for that foul thing in your hand, it will not shed a drop of my blood."

"Three of your minions lie dead in the dark, and nothing will keep you from the same fate," Blackwood took another step forward, his senses heightened.

"Children," the witch crowed, her voice rising to a horrible tone, and for a moment her beautiful face twisted into something hideous. All around the chamber, the dragon candles erupted with brilliant flames. Magic crackled through the air.

"Your coven is destroyed, and I won't allow you to take the girl," the inquisitor declared.

The witch glanced at Mary Shaw. "Coven," she laughed again, the cackle rolling from the depths of her chest. "Is that what you think this is? The gathering of a coven? How foolish of you," she sneered. The witch stood up from her haunches and stretched her back and arms luxuriously, as if the presence of an inquisitor gave her little concern. Blackwood looked past the arrogance and yet he could see no worry in the witch. A voice of alarm whispered in the back of his mind. *Something is not right.* He quickly shoved it aside.

The witch walked over to Mary Shaw and ran her fingers through the girl's long black hair. "She is my daughter, can't you see that," the witch teased, her golden eyes flaring dangerously in the candlelight. "Those three girls in the dark were my daughters too."

"We see the stealing of village girls differently," said Blackwood flatly, slowly taking another step toward the she-devil. Witches were treacherous foes—fragile and easy enough to dispatch if one managed to get close—but they could strike like a snake. The inquisitor advanced cautiously.

"*We*," the witch spat the word out. "We? You mean the Citadel? The Inquisition? The world of man? How dare you tell me how *you* see the world. I've seen how differently you see the world."

Blackwood allowed the witch to speak, taking another careful step forward. He was slowly whittling away at the distance between them.

The witch turned Mary Shaw around to face Blackwood and ran the tip of the bone talon along the girl's chin, her golden eyes smiling greedily at the inquisitor. The girl was frozen in the witch's enchantment, her eyes white and unseeing. "You see this as stealing, no … Wait. In your tongue the word is *kidnap*. You see this as kidnap. I see it as reclamation."

The dragon candles flared again, dispelling all shadow from the chamber. The vision of Megen rolled through Blackwood's mind again. The great fire consuming the town. The Baldirim on the hilltop. The seven women tied to stakes and put to death in the dark of the night. As the images raced behind his eyes, he could sense the witch standing on the edge of the light cast by the burning pyres. The dank underground air gave way to the smell of smoke souring the fresh hilltop air. He could see the eyes of the girl tied to the stake, staring at him through the flames that ravaged her. He could see her face in the hellish light and saw Mary Shaw. *Children. Mother.* As quickly as the vision erupted in his mind, Blackwood found himself back in the witch's chamber.

"Impossible," he muttered. Again, the feeling of wickedness came to mind.

"But possible in the *Old Ways*," the witch countered.

The tale of Megen and that of the Seven Sisters was at least a century old. The witch grinned, revealing the hideous line of black teeth again, and laughed as if she could see the disbelief blooming in Blackwood's thoughts. "You do not believe that I can be the same witch who gave birth to those executed in Megen." The witch's eyes flashed malevolently.

"No witch that old still lives," Blackwood barked. "Your words are lies, and I'll hear no more of it. You will die in this room and the girl will be saved from your schemes." The inquisitor took a bold step forward and raised the *sharur* before him. The witch's eyes flickered with the first sign of concern at the sharpened edge of the hallowed weapon.

She pointed the bone talon at the symbol of the Inquisition hanging from Blackwood's neck and hissed. "There is plenty the Citadel knows nothing of," she taunted. "Take the girl from me you may, but I will have my children back. A storm is coming and the black tower of Gotheim will fall beneath its weight. Heed my words, hunter."

"The Citadel will stand for a thousand years," Blackwood growled. "Now suffer its judgement," he declared …

* * *

Fee barely felt the arm of Blackwood come across his chest. He could scarcely remember walking into the brightly lit chamber for that matter. Mary Shaw stood somewhere to the side, out of sight like a phantom. Blackwood was beside him, but it felt like the inquisitor was miles away. He could hear Blackwood's voice in the distance, like a murmur on the back of a distant wind. The only thing that seemed real was the woman before him. He knew it was the witch, but he could feel nothing but adoration for her. It nearly bordered on worship. She transfixed him as she rose to her feet. Locks of black hair fell across her bare chest almost all the way to her navel. She slowly approached him, her longs legs moving in supple strides beneath the worn dress that hung from her hips. Golden eyes shone brilliantly from the band of black charcoal across her face. "I can see your thoughts, pup," she crooned. Fee could not take his eyes from her. Every movement of her body was a temptation. Inside his mind he tried to resist her, recalling her true appearance—the twisted and gnarled hag of the fog; the hideous wretch from the inn. Her true appearance. *Or had that all been an illusion? Was this an illusion?* He couldn't be sure. His mind was in conflict, his thoughts devouring each other like rapacious wolves. *As long as they are still your thoughts.* Blackwood's words spoke to him, but the inquisitor's voice was soft and weak against the growing presence of the witch. She was quickly taking hold in his mind, infecting every thought. Even the ceaseless pain from the spider bites had become nothing more than an irritation.

"You thirst after me," she whispered, her bare feet stepping lightly across the stone ground. "I can see it in your mind," she cooed.

Carnal thoughts punctuated Fee's mind. Feral visions pulsed violently in his head—visions of he and the witch becoming one. He could feel the pleasure of the witch on top of him, as well as the pain within his soul as her magic consumed him and drained him of his essence. Her lips tasted sweet, her breath was unbearable, his body flew and his soul crumbled into dust. Both death and life mingled within him as the witch took him for herself—wilderness consuming his humanity. Fee tried to fight the onslaught, but a dampening fatigue was beginning to encroach on the fringes of his mind and he could feel his willpower slip.

In the distance, as if beyond the horizon, Fee could hear Blackwood speak. *We see the stealing of village girls differently.*

The inquisitor's voice was foreign like something beyond the dream state he found himself in. Fee pushed against it, but a white-hot lance of pain shot through his thoughts.

"Don't deny it," the witch whispered. She was upon him now, her one hand sliding across his shoulder, whilst the other drew the point of a bone talon down his cheek. He could smell her now. She carried the scent of dark earth, rich and raw, and beneath it there was the smell of filth—like foul feathers and decay.

"Begone," he managed. Another lance of pain bolted through his body and he could feel the tip of the bone talon cut into the side of his face as the witch pressed it against his skin.

"No," she whispered into his ear. He tried to recoil from

the smell of death that came from her mouth. "It's been so long since I've enjoyed a young man like yourself." Another series of perverted scenes flashed through his mind. *Exhilaration and annihilation. Rapture and doom.* He could feel the oiliness of the witch's power consume him. There was a sweetness to her, a taste, he could not deny, but the wretchedness of her being also sickened him.

Blackwood's voice echoed from the depths of some other realm, *Impossible.*

It all seemed impossible to Fee. The witch circled him, walking around his back, dragging the bone talon across his shoulders. He could feel its tip cut through his shirt and draw blood from his skin. *Pain and pleasure.*

The witch leaned over his shoulder and a thick tongue, purple and wet, crawled from her mouth and licked a drop of blood from one of the oozing spider bites on Fee's neck. "He will try and take the girl from me," she whispered.

Fee's eyes followed her finger as it pointed to Blackwood, who now stood a few feet away from him. The inquisitor seemed to be confronting someone, but he could not see. *Had he not been speaking to the witch?* Nothing seemed to make sense. The only constant was her voice. The tip of the grotesque tongue reached into his ear and the witch sighed a soft breath of air. The sickening smell of it filled his nose and yet he wanted more. He could feel it consume his head like a noxious cloud and the chamber slipped into a blur. Ahead of him only Blackwood remained clear. "You must stop him, Fee," the witch insisted. "You must help me."

Fee suddenly became aware of both the dagger and pistol in his hands.

Now suffer its judgement. The inquisitor's voice boomed through the chamber like thunder.

"You must stop him," the witch hissed into his ear.

* * *

"Now suffer its judgement," Blackwood bellowed. He'd grown tired of the witch's lies. His duty was to bring the fiend to its destruction and not to listen to its black reasoning. He lunged forward with the *sharur*, willing the weapon into the form of a spear. Energy crackled through the fibre of the *sharur's* living wood and the weapon extended into a pole-arm as it flew through the air towards the witch's throat. A deafening thunder exploded in the chamber and something hot cut through his left shoulder, sending him reeling. The spear sailed wide, missing the witch and burying its tip into a heap of dragon candles against the wall. Blackwood turned, pulling the spear from the mound of wax, and saw Fee pointing the four-shot revolver at him. Blue smoke trailed from the gun's barrel. The witch now stood behind the young apprentice, her long tongue slithering back into her smirking mouth, like a bloated snake. Her golden eyes glared at Blackwood with nothing but hate.

"Fee," Blackwood cried, looking his apprentice and the witch. Already a strong stream of warm blood flowed from the wound in his shoulder and a searing pain ran through the bones of his arm, but he still managed to hold a tight fist around the black coin in his palm.

Fee pulled the trigger of the revolver again. There was nothing but a hollow click. Apprentice and master stared at each other for a moment, before Fee charged forward.

"Fee don't do this," Blackwood yelled again, but his apprentice would not listen. The young man ran toward him, eyes distant and elsewhere, dagger drawn and ready to strike.

Suddenly from the rear, two pale arms reached around Blackwood's neck and pulled him off-stance. *Mary Shaw.* The witch's horrible laugh echoed off the walls of the chamber and the dragon candles burned furiously. The inquisitor regained his balance against the surprise attack from Mary Shaw and threw his head back like a hammer. The hard crest of his skull crashed into the softness of Mary's face and the loud crack of bone filled his ears. He didn't hesitate. Blackwood looked over his shoulder and saw the girl reeling backwards, torrents of crimson blood pouring from her broken nose. He swung his arm around, gritting through the pain in his shoulder, and buried the back of his clenched fist into the girl's left temple. Mary Shaw toppled over, bouncing off a row of candles and hitting the ground with a heavy thud.

In the meantime, Fee had closed the ground between them and he was almost upon the inquisitor. Blackwood turned the first lunge from Fee with a well-timed parry from the pole-arm of the *sharur* spear. Fee turned immediately and swiped across the inquisitor's chest. The blade of the dagger flashed brightly with candlelight. Blackwood blocked again and pushed the young man back with a forceful shove.

"Listen to my voice," Blackwood pleaded. "Remember who you are. Remember your name."

Fee looked at him blankly, his face bereft of any youth. A fine cut ran down his cheek and a fresh line of blood trickled from it. Black rings circled his reddened eyes and the pallor of his face screamed of the dead. A dark layer of grime stained the side of his head where the witch's tongue had cast its spell. *Enchantment.* The young man was under the witch's influence, and the only way to free him was to kill the witch or inflict a harsh measure of pain upon his apprentice.

Blackwood looked to the side and saw the witch stalking him from across the chamber. The mesmerising beauty of her face was now mangled with the hungering anticipation of his death. An evil glee filled her eyes as she enjoyed the inquisitor's contemplations. Blackwood was beginning to doubt his ability to defeat this witch, especially without the aid of his apprentice, but even if he were to save Fee, the young man would certainly be in no condition to fight once freed from the witch's spell. He gritted his teeth at the choices on offer.

"Do you hear me, Fee?" Blackwood called again, hoping his apprentice would hear his voice through the murk of whatever magic held him to the witch's will.

The apprentice remained silent but answered with an advancing step, the dagger held ready for another attack.

The inquisitor clenched his jaw and fortified his resolve. "Forgive me, young boy," he whispered. "Perhaps one day you'll be grateful for what I'm going to do."

Fee launched himself at the inquisitor again, his arm drawn high ready to bring the dagger down in a long sweeping action at his master's face. It was a wild move. An impractical move against the likes of an inquisitor. Blackwood took a step back and, according to his will, the *sharur* shifted back into the form of a longsword. In one fluid move, too quick to follow, Blackwood met Fee's attack with the edge of the longsword *sharur* and separated hand from arm. Fee let out a harsh, guttural cry as he fell to the floor clutching the stump at the end of his arm, and the witch crowed with laughter.

Before Blackwood could turn to face her, the witch was upon him, sailing through the air like a black blur. Golden eyes and wicked teeth leered at him as her long brown fingers reaching for him. Blackwood was knocked from his feet by the force of the charge and landed heavily against the stone ground. The witch fell on top of him, crouching on his chest, one long thumb already digging into the bullet wound in his shoulder. A fresh wave of pain ran through his arm. He tried to raise his other arm and bring the *sharur* upon the witch, but the she-devil already had it pinned with her other hand. The strength in her slim body was deceiving. She held him fixed in place, her body pressed against his, unable to break free. She leaned down to his face and met his dark eyes with her penetrating golden orbs. "Weren't you going to kill me, hunter," she teased. She stretched open her mouth and the thick, purple tongue leapt out and licked Blackwood's face. "Now I will kill you," she said, her words carrying, despite the horrible tongue writhing from her open mouth. "Or perhaps I should curse your soul, child-killer. Death is a gift for you. You and your kind deserve to be hunted, like we've been hunted. I know what I'll do," a sickly laugh rolled out of her, almost childish but evil. "I'll mark you, hunter," she buried her thumb deeper into the hole in his shoulder. "I'll mark you for my kin, so that you will be pursued until your last days on this earth. The children of the *fae* will hunt your body and your soul. What do you say to that, inquisitor?" the witch sneered. Blackwood met her golden eyes and said nothing. He held his resolve and began to shift the black coin in his hand.

* * *

Remember your name. Pain, worse than he ever experienced, pulled Fee from the dream-like state. At first there was only a smoky haze, but the burning agony at the end of his arm brought the stoney ground into focus. Cold sweat soaked through his shirt, and weakness racked his body. His head was swimming and he struggled to gain focus. He rolled over and looked at the end of his arm and saw nothing but a clean end, and a rhythmic bubbling of blood from the gaping wound. A few feet from where he found himself, he saw his hand laying in the dirt, the dagger still held between pale, dead fingers. He had no memory of what happened, except that the voice of the witch was no longer in his mind. He could no longer feel her oily presence on his soul. Fee's vision blurred and he retched on himself. In his other hand he still held the pistol. A struggle across the floor drew his attention. To the side he saw Mary Shaw sprawled against the edge of the chamber wall—whether she was alive or not, he couldn't tell. A few feet from her, Blackwood was pinned against the ground, the witch perched upon his chest, whispering to him in some foul language. *Fae-tongue*. The she-devil's thick tongue coiled like a snake between their faces and she seemed to be tormenting a wound in his master's shoulder.

Fee gathered what senses remained to him, and courage too, and flicked the cylinder of the revolver open. *Empty*. He was sure there was one shot left. He dropped the gun to the ground and, with his remaining hand, pulled a pouch of bullets from the inside pocket of his coat. He fumbled for a bullet, dropping one to the ground and scrounging in the dirt to get a firm grip on it. After what seemed like an age, he finally managed to grab hold of the bullet and clumsily slipped it into one of the four empty chambers. Blackwood groaned, and Fee could make out the skin-crawling snicker of the witch. His master needed him. He snapped the cylinder back into revolver frame with a violent twist of his wrist and took comfort in the warm click of metal against metal. Lifting the pistol, Fee leaned on his mutilated arm, wincing in agony, fighting against the darkness around the edges of his vision, and took aim at the witch upon Blackwood. He steadied his irregular breathing for a moment and took a long breath as he took aim down the barrel of the revolver—the spot between the witch's shoulders marked.

* * *

The gunshot filled the chamber with another deafening roar and two feathers from the witch's crown were obliterated by the passing bullet. The witch turned from Blackwood and screamed at the beleaguered man lying in the dirt. The inquisitor needn't look to know Fee had somehow—*by the grace of the emperors*—managed to fire another round from his revolver. Blackwood took advantage of the distraction and lifted the hand holding the coin and pressed it between the breasts of the witch, firmly placing the black token against her skin. Immediately the coin took on the weight of a heavy stone as it pulled at the magic in the she-devil and turned frighteningly cold. The weight of the coin bore down on his wounded shoulder, but Blackwood held it in place. If they were going to escape, he had no other choice. The witch cried in pain and whipped around, her golden eyes burning with anger. The dragon candles erupted, sending bright shards of light upward, illuminating the witch's face. Dark, twisting lines pulled at her skin, turning her striking looks into a mask of nightmares. She grabbed the wrist of the hand that held the black coin, letting go of Blackwood's other hand—the one that held the *sharur*. In an instant, Blackwood willed a long needle-like form from the polished handle and drove it up and buried it between the witch's ribs. The grotesque, pythonic tongue snapped back into the witch's mouth and she released a terrifying wail. Blackwood met her eyes, the power and hate in those golden orbs dissolving into fear and panic. The dragon candles turned into furnaces, black wax retreating beneath the growing heat, and a wind gathering in the chamber, unsettling and carrying the dirt from the ground. The dust swirled along the walls, turning into a stinging whirlwind. Fee buried his face into the pit of his arm, but Blackwood held the coin to the witch's chest and did not let go of the *sharur*.

The wind howled and the whirlwind turned faster, pulling more dirt into the coiling air. The dust-devil gathered around the witch, concealing her completely in a shifting gyre of sand, and, as quickly as it gathered, the wind died and the maelstrom disintegrated. Silence crept into the underground chamber. The strange figures and ornaments hanging from the ceiling swung violently in the wake of the phantom wind. Blackwood sat up from the ground, the wound on his side and the bullet hole in his shoulder disagreeing with the movement. Fee looked at him from across the chamber, bewildered and relieved at the sudden stillness.

"Is she dead?" The question was more of a plea from the battered apprentice.

Blackwood looked at the dragon candles around the chamber—not one had been extinguished—and he felt a heavy darkness settle on his heart. "Just gone," he said hoarsely.

10

THE FOG CLEARS

The journey back to Westgrave was a beleaguered one. Blackwood and Fee trudged through the forest with the unconscious Mary Shaw between them. Fee, with his incapacitated arm bound with the makeshift tourniquet that was Blackwood's belt, had his right arm swung around the girl's waist, while the inquisitor supported from the left. The early light of dawn had begun to sneak through the canopy of the trees by the time they left the cave and, as they crossed the tree line between the woods and the village, the day seemed less gloomy. The fog that besieged the village was nearly gone and, for the first time, Blackwood could survey the settlement with clarity. The cobbled street was narrower than the fog had made him to believe and the houses running along each side of the singular road were simple abodes. Further down, the inn towered over everything else as the only two-storied building in the village. The village folk had gathered in the road to wonder at the sudden break in the fog when the three survivors emerged from the woods. Frightened stares and gaping mouths followed as they pushed through the last stretch to the inn. Most barely recognised Fee as the young gentleman who had spent nearly a fortnight in their village. Swollen spider bites, a bloody stump lassoed by a leather belt and his weathered face gave him the appearance of a war casualty stricken by a skin pox. Others gasped at Mary Shaw, her face bloodied and nose bent, being carried between the two strangers from Gotheim. None dared to look at the inquisitor. His wide brimmed hat covered most of his face with a dark shadow, but the terrible strength that remained his eyes was awful to look at. Blood still glistened from the wound in his shoulder and his hands were cut and bruised, his clothes torn and dirtied. The *sharur* was back in its holster, concealed beneath his coat. Although no one met the inquisitor's glare or had the courage to look upon his hard face, the village folk of Westgrave all stared at the black candle he carried in his free hand. The candle was thick enough that the man's fingers could not reach around and touch each other, and the flame that burned at the end of the wick seemed untroubled by the gentle breeze that blew the fog away. It was a dragon candle, something none of the people of Westgrave would be familiar with. Blackwood ignored their gawking stares and ordered Fee to hurry for the inn.

They would catch the next train from Westgrave, mid-morning the next day. Blackwood had retreated to his room and had decided not to leave it until it was time for the train. He'd tended to Fee's wound, cauterising the stump with a clothes iron heated in the hearth downstairs, and the young man now slept in the feathered bed of his own room. As for Mary Shaw, the inquisitor allowed her mother to wash the grime and blood from her, but the girl had not yet awoken. It made no difference to Blackwood. Awake or asleep, tomorrow would be the last morning the girl spent in Westgrave. He would be taking the girl back to Gotheim. To the Citadel to be exact. If his inquisitor's intuition was right

—*and it* had never failed him—there would be much he could learn from the girl. She had been bound to the witch, and there was no knowing what the she-devil had inadvertently transferred to the girl.

Once both Fee and Mary Shaw had been taken care of, in the common room of *The Candle and Cask*, Blackwood told the people of Westgrave about the cave in the woods, and of the three girls he was forced to kill, for they were under the power of the *Old Ways*. To a hushed audience, he related the news of the witch. He said nothing of the witch's escape but told the village folk that they had been freed from the fiend's clutches and that the Inquisition's business was at an end in Westgrave. At this, the people sighed a unified breath of relief.

In the darkness of his room, Blackwood sat on the edge of the bed and tended to his own wounds. He'd taken what linen was left from wrapping Fee's arm and bandaged his shoulder. A violent bruise had formed along his ribs from where the witching girl had struck him and he was certain one or two bones had been broken. Perched on top of the table in the room, stood the dragon candle—its everlasting flame burning silently, unmoving and unchanging. He had severely wounded the witch, burying the long blade of the *sharur* into her ribs but the dragon candle burned strongly. As long as its flame burned, he knew the witch was still alive. He tied the ends of the bandage around his shoulder, leaned back onto the bed and rested his head against the wall. He clenched his jaw against the pain in his side and watched the dragon candle burn, the flame hovering against the darkness. The night was quiet and there was little sound in the inn. Even the common room was still. A foreboding weighed heavily on Blackwood's heart. A dread that kept him from sleeping. The witch was gone. Its prey lay asleep in the room next door, in possession of secrets that only time would reveal. Yet, these were not the sources of his distress. The candle remained constant in the darkness and Blackwood closed his eyes, the silhouette of the flame still bright against the back of his lids.

As long as the dragon candle burned, he would hunt the witch, for he was an inquisitor of the Citadel.

As long as its flame burned, he would be hunted, for in his secret heart, he knew he was cursed.

ACKNOWLEDGMENTS

Blackwood did not emerge from the grim darkness without the aid of others. Nor did the shadows and devilry that lurk amongst the countless spires of Gotheim. The realm of the *fae* and the burgeoning conspiracy of the Lord Marshal's Citadel and the Bishop King's Church (all which is still to come in future tales) have been a product of conversations and concept proofing with an indispensable few, who were willing to take the first steps into a gothic world of nightmares, grotesque creatures and a struggle of darkness against darkness. As I have mentioned, Blackwood and Gotheim were not what I had intended to write when I first sat down with the endeavour to write a fantasy series, and I feel - as clichéd as it may sound - that Gotheim found and chose me.

Thank you to Roxy, who allowed me to disappear from the world and explore the realm of Gotheim in my isolation, and for pushing me back into a regime of creation when fatigue threatened to overcome me. For believing. For motivating. For cracking the whip. Without this support, I doubt Gotheim would have become what it is.

As an incredibly grateful writer, I want to thank Lynne

Davis and Diane Coetzee for crafting and moulding my rough words into the polished body of work that it is today. Thank you to my beta-readers: Roland, Caitlyn and Chris.

Lastly, thank you to Waldo Buchner, who took my simple briefs and created incredible visual components for Gotheim - bringing the world to life, and making it look as vivid and insidious as I imagined it.

- Clyde Davis, June 27, 2019

ABOUT THE AUTHOR

Clyde Davis continues to develop his appetites for literature - exploring both literary fiction and fantasy - and has found the attraction in both. As a writer, he swings between both genres, often looking for the point where they meet. His writing combines the realism of fiction with the magical elements of fantasy, lending aspects from one genre to give a unique impression on the other. With this as his core principle, Clyde refuses to isolate himself to any genre. He enjoys inhabiting both worlds, and is a firm believer that a writer can move between realms, pursuing inspiration as it comes. According to Clyde, the process of creation is intrinsic to the human condition, no matter the complexity or form. Whether it's a conversation or a novel, we are all born with the ability to tell tales and be creative. It is only in the way that it is told that makes us different.

Clyde's works are eclectic and varied and he strives to offer his readers tales from every corner of his creativity.